RATPOCALYPSE

RATPOCALYPSE

Scott M. Baker

Also by Scott M. Baker

Novels

A World Gone Dark
A World Gone Dark II
It Came From the Desert
OSS: Office of Supernatural Services
Operation Majestic
Nurse Alissa vs. the Zombies
Nurse Alissa vs. the Zombies: Escape
Nurse Alissa vs. the Zombies III: Firestorm
Nurse Alissa vs. the Zombies IV: Hunters
Nurse Alissa vs. the Zombies V: Desperate Mission
Nurse Alissa vs. the Zombies VI: Rescue
Nurse Alissa vs. the Zombies VII: On the Road
Nurse Alissa vs. the Zombies VIII: New Beginnings
Nurse Alissa vs. the Zombies IX: Calm Before the Storm
Nurse Alissa vs. the Zombies X: Endgame
The Chronicles of Paul: A Nurse Alissa Spin-Off
The Chronicles of Paul II: Errand of Mercy
The Chronicle of Paul III: Road to Nowhere
The Ghosts of Eden Hollow
The Ghosts of Salem Village
The Ghosts of the Maria Doria
The Ghosts of Bethlehem Asylum
The Ghosts of Treblinka
Frozen World
Shattered World I: Paris
Shattered World II: Russia
Shattered World III: China
Shattered World IV: Japan

Shattered World V: Hell
The Vampire Hunters
Vampyrnomicon
Dominion
Rotter World
Rotter Nation
Rotter Apocalypse

Novellas

Nazi Ghouls From Space
Twilight of the Living Dead
This Is Why We Can't Have Nice Things During the Zombie Apocalypse
Dead Water

Anthologies

Cruise of the Living Dead and Other Stories
Incident on Ironstone Lane and Other Horror Stories
Crossroads in the Dark V: Beyond the Borders
Rejected for Content
Roots of a Beating Heart
The Zombie Road Fan Fiction Collection
The Collector
Vlada: Tales of the Damned
Through the Aftermath: A Post-Apocalyptic Anthology
Time of the Undead

A Schattenseite Book

Ratpocalypse
by S M. Baker.

Print Edition
ISBN-13: 979-8-9884973-9-4

To the students at Kreiva Public Charter School

It was a pleasure and an honor to be your teacher for two years.
I enjoyed every minute with you.
I wish you all success and happiness in your future.

PROLOGUE

THE OUTBREAK OCCURRED five years ago, though no one knew for certain how it began. At least, no one who survived.

A few people vaguely remember news reports about a zombie outbreak near Wuhan, Hubei Province, China. Some remembered hearing that the outbreak occurred in Wuhan while others swore the virus erupted in a small village several hundred kilometers from the city. No one could recall if the report came from an Internet source or a TV news station. Except for a few conservative journalists and a bunch of conspiracy theorists, everyone thought the story was a hoax.

In hindsight, the world should have paid attention.

Eleven days later, the zombie virus erupted in major metropolitan areas across the United States. Within three days, the outbreak spread to the surrounding neighborhoods and suburbs. Washington prohibited domestic and international flights to and from America. It took more than a week for those fleeing the outbreaks to reach the countryside and establish safe havens. By the third week, most of the nation had been overrun by the living dead.

The virus then broke out in Hong Kong and Shanghai. Beijing immediately canceled all air travel and placed the nation under martial law.

Two days later, the virus erupted in Mongolia, Siberia, Kazakhstan, and Myanmar. Air travel worldwide was suspended.

By the end of the month, every nation reported instances of the zombie virus. Billions were turned from the living to the living dead. Major cities collapsed within forty-eight hours.

Nine months after the first reported case, pockets of humanity began to fight back, exterminating the living dead and slowly retaking lost territory. The discovery in Boston of a zombie virus vaccine that prevented those being bitten from turning offered the advantage mankind needed to wage war against the dead.

Several nations, including the United States, opted to isolate the major cities rather than retake them, realizing the risks far outweighed the minimal gains. The government-in-exile in New Mexico made the decision to wait several years, let the hordes in major population centers rot away, then cleanse the cities of the once-human detritus.

Ten months ago, the last of the living dead in North America outside the isolation zones was eliminated. No outbreaks had occurred since then. News from around the globe, though minimal due to the loss of satellite communications, indicated that other nations had achieved the same level of success.

For the survivors in the United States, a sense of ease settled over the rural populations. Then began the struggle to rebuild their lives. Townships sprouted up, and people lived as their ancestors had generations ago—growing their own food and producing by hand any materials they needed to survive. Civilization slowly returned to normal.

What no one foresaw was the new nightmare about to unfold.

Animals remained immune to the zombie virus. Millions had been bitten or devoured by the living dead, but none had reanimated. Within months of the initial outbreak, major population centers had been overtaken by colonies of rats, in many cases numbering in the millions. With humans gone, and with no trash to feed on, they burrowed into apartments and homes in search of anything edible. Little remained. Once the typical sources of food had been devoured, they began feeding off the carcasses of the living dead that had succumbed to time and starvation, and occasionally on the few still staggering along the streets. Inspection teams sent into Chicago, Los Angeles, and New York City reported rats stripping the bodies clean, which would make the humans' job easier when the decision would finally be made to reclaim the cities.

However, in Boston, an unforeseen event occurred in a scenario that was possible yet highly improbable.

The zombie virus species jumped from one of the human corpses to the rat feeding on it, an enormous rat the size of a dog, measuring four feet in length from its nose to the tips of its tail. Maybe its immense size made the rodent vulnerable to the virus, or maybe it had an unusual DNA structure. Not that it mattered. It became infected with the zombie virus, beginning a new nightmare.

Once the rat morphed, it began consuming the only other available food: the rest of the colony. The virus rapidly spread amongst the rodent population, creating several million zombie rats in desperate need of food. With nothing left in Boston to feed on, the colony had only one option.

To migrate out of the city in search of sustenance.

CHAPTER ONE

BRAD MILLER STOOD on the back deck of his house on the east side of Nahant Island overlooking the ocean. The horizon glowed yellow, a prelude to the coming sunrise. Brad sighed contentedly. He loved dawn, watching the rays of light as they spread across the water's surface, reflecting off the waves and creating a dazzling kaleidoscope of nature. It was his favorite moment of the day.

At least it was until five years ago when the zombie outbreak nearly caused the extinction of mankind.

In Massachusetts, the virus first erupted in Boston and spread to the suburbs. Within forty-eight hours, the horde of living dead reached Nahant. Despite the residents erecting a barricade across the causeway connecting the mainland to the island, the living dead swarmed over the defenses and overran the entire island in less than an hour. Those not immediately taken down desperately made their way to the shore, hoping to find some means of salvation, instead being forced to choose between swimming to a safety that no longer existed, drowning, or being eaten alive. Only a handful escaped—a boat with six people heading north, three teenagers on jet skis, a family of four in a rickety rowboat, and Brad. Grabbing a canoe from his neighbor's backyard, he paddled his way along the coast until he found a safe place to go ashore. That was two days later in Rockport, thirty miles north of Nahant.

The next few years were a nightmare Brad desperately tried to forget, pushing down the memories only to have his subconscious dredge them back to the surface. Months surviving on his own, scrounging for what little food he could scavenge, avoiding the living dead that wanted to devour him and the living who wanted to kill him for his supplies. Settling down in a community of survivors, only to have it swarmed over a few weeks later by a stampede of zombies. Eventually, joining one of the ad hoc units that, in coordination with hundreds of others across the country, initiated the nationwide sweep that eventually cleansed the United States. And finally, the battle to contain the living dead inside of Boston, a terrifying operation that succeeded only after three weeks of non-stop conflict and at the cost of thousands of lives. With New England secure, Brad resigned from the unit and returned to Nahant, hoping to rebuild his life on the fond memories of the distant past.

Ironically, the island collapsed so quickly that only a few buildings suffered no structural damage. A few bullet holes along the front façade of his house were the only signs of the conflict. However, four years of being unattended had taken their toll. Not that it mattered. Brad was home, and the repairs and cleaning gave him something to do in his free time.

"Good morning, Birthday Boy."

Brad smiled as Sadie Cummings cuddled against his back and slid her arms around his chest, hugging him. Sadie was the only good thing to enter his life during the zombie apocalypse. They met when she joined the cleansing unit three weeks after him. Sadie refused to tell him anything about her experiences, which he completely understood. They became good friends. During the disastrous operation along the Charles River, when a pack of zombies overran the advancing forces, Sadie nearly died when a dozen of the living dead trapped her in a Humvee. Brad rescued her and led both of them to safety. After that, they became lovers. Both resigned on the same day and moved to Nahant to begin what would hopefully be a better life.

Brad placed his hands over Sadie's and squeezed lovingly.

"Are you sure it's my birthday? We've lost all track of time."

"It's close enough."

"Thank you for remembering."

"I did more than remember. I got you something."

"You didn't have to do that."

"I wanted to."

Clasping his hand, Sadie led him away from the window and to the dining room table. A blue pillowcase covered his gift. Brad stopped in front of the table as she moved to the side and placed her hand on the edge of the pillowcase.

"Close your eyes."

Brad chuckled. "Seriously?"

"Do you want your gift?"

He smiled. "Of course."

"Then close your eyes." Sadie said each word slowly as if chastising a disobedient child.

Brad complied. A few seconds later, Sadie said, "Okay. You can open them."

When he did, his mouth dropped open. A 750 ml bottle of Maker's Mark whiskey and three cigars sat in the center of the table.

"Are you surprised?"

"Very. Where did you get these?"

"Ethan. His scavenger team found a huge cache of alcohol and cigars in someone's house in Gloucester that had not been ransacked. When I mentioned your birthday was coming up, he gave this to me for free. He said it was the least he could do considering everything you've done for the community."

Brad stared at the gift in amazement.

Sadie's grin faded. "Don't you like them?"

"It's the second-best thing to happen to me since the outbreak."

"What's the first?"

"You."

Sadie rushed forward and jumped into his arms. "I love

you so much."

They kissed passionately. When Brad let Sadie down, she took his hand and pulled him toward the bedroom.

"Really?" asked Brad.

"It's part of your birthday gift."

"This early?"

"If we do it tonight, your breath will smell like cigar smoke." Sadie smiled and winked. "I love you, but there are limits."

"JESUS, ETHAN." TED Donnelly, one of Nahant's deputies, stared into the bed of the golf cart, his eyes wide in disbelief. "Where did you find this?"

"This" referred to a special stash of items resting in two white plastic crates: sixteen bottles of whiskey, including Jack Daniel's, Maker's Mark, Baker's Bourbon, Jim Beam, and several others, as well as twenty-six boxes of cigars.

Ethan Wright smiled. "My scavenger team found them in an abandoned mansion in Gloucester. The owner had set up a small cigar lounge in the back of the place. We lucked out. Paul almost passed by the room, only spotting it on the way out."

"We're going to get a lot for this stuff." Sheriff Terry O'Brien lifted a bottle of Jack Daniel's out of the container and studied it. "I can't remember the last time I had a shot of whiskey."

"Keep the bottle and a box of cigars for yourself."

O'Brien's eyes lit up like a child walking into the living room on Christmas morning. "Are you serious?"

"After all the work you've put in, you deserve it."

O'Brien removed a box of cigars, brought the gifts over to his Land Rover, and hid them under a blanket in the back seat.

Ethan pondered how much things had changed, going from good to nightmare to better.

Five years ago, Ethan was the CEO of a tech company based in Portland, Maine, worth $100 million. He owned a huge house on the coast and a summer home in Florida. His company thrived because he took good care of his employees, just shy of one hundred staff, offering them good pay and benefits. Most importantly, he had married a beautiful, intelligent, and loyal wife who had given him two teenage boys. At the age of forty-three, he could not have asked for a better life.

That life came crashing down around him in less than a day.

The zombie virus that broke out in Portland consumed the city in less than twenty-four hours. Fortunately for Ethan, he was on a private plane bound for Chicago on a business trip. Had he been in Portland, he would have more than likely died while trying to escape the city, as he assumed all of his employees had. The pilot landed at a small airport near Rochester, New York. Ethan began his nightmare from there.

Unfortunately for his family, they were on vacation in Italy at the time. His wife called, her voice croaking from fear and anxiety, to tell him that she and the kids were boarding the last flight out of Rome, heading for New York City, and pleaded with him to meet her there. Ethan never heard from them again.

Ethan's life followed the same pattern as everyone else who survived the outbreak. He traveled the countryside on his own, trying to survive while avoiding being eaten by the living dead, eventually teaming up with one of the many units cleansing the country. His last assignment took him to Boston, where he had helped clean out the suburbs and isolate the city. Once his tour of duty ended, he considered going back to Portland but opted not to since too many heartbreaking memories were associated with the area. Instead, he stayed in Massachusetts, eventually settling in Nahant, choosing this location not because of its scenic view, but due to the fact it would be next to impossible for anyone to raid the island since it was connected to land by a causeway.

That's when his life entered its upward swing.

Ethan joined the town council, a group of five residents, including O'Brien, who met frequently to discuss ways to rebuild their community. By then, power had been restored to several cities along the coast, including Nahant, which provided electricity and water pumps to locals. However, the food supply remained dangerously low. Ethan suggested revitalizing the fishing industry and turning the Flash Road Park and Kelly Greens Golf Course into agricultural farms. By the end of the first summer, the island had produced enough food so not only was it self-sufficient, but it had plenty to spare. The council wanted to hoard the surplus until Ethan pointed out that most of it would spoil within weeks. He suggested setting up a barter station at the far end of the causeway, which would not only help sustain other communities that had been established nearby but might also provide them with other goods in short supply. The council approved his idea. Within a month, the pickup truck used to carry the supplies had evolved into a small tent city used by seven towns for trading and had been given the nickname Barterville.

Soon, those who came to Barterville began asking for items such as over-the-counter medications, batteries, books, and clothes. Ethan got the idea to send groups of scavengers in search of these "luxuries." The rules were simple: only abandoned residences were to be searched; no personal items, such as photo albums and jewelry, could be confiscated; and bringing back any illegal drugs was forbidden. Once word got out about the new stash of tradable items, business doubled. People began making requests that his scavenger teams did their best to fulfill. One of his teams brought back a cache of porno magazines, X-rated DVDs, and sex toys, which were cleaned out in an afternoon.

The past several months made Ethan feel useful again. Not

only had he succeeded in making Nahant self-sufficient and aided the surrounding communities in their survival, but his scavengers provided everyone with a sense of satisfaction, allowing them to realize that life was slowly returning to a new normal. Ethan felt prouder of his efforts on Nahant than when he ran the multi-million-dollar corporation in Maine, because here he helped an entire community. His efforts to improve the lives of those who relied on him helped fill the void left behind by the loss of his family.

Two months ago, when the town council decided to elect a mayor, Ethan's name was added to the ballot, and he won with ninety-three percent of the votes.

"We'll bring these to Barterville tomorrow," said Donnelly. "Is there anything in particular we should be trading for it?"

"There's a list on a clipboard in the city hall's lobby. I checked it this morning. The residents are asking for lots of stuff, mostly luxuries. Melissa updated it this morning. Take it with you and see what you can trade for. I trust you."

"No problem." Donnelly placed the lids back on the containers. "Is there anything special you want?"

Ethan thought about it for a moment, then shook his head. What he really wanted was lost years ago in Italy. "I have everything I need."

"WHAT IS NINE times eight?" asked Alanna.

The class stared at her as if she had grown a second head.

"Come on, guys. This is easy."

Kevin snorted. "It's easy for you. You're old."

Alanna placed her hands on her hip, suppressing a smile. "I'm only sixteen."

"That's old compared to us," joked Monica, who was eleven.

"Really?" asked Liz, the middle-aged head of the school,

who entered at that moment. "What does that make me?"

"Ancient," replied Kevin with a chuckle.

Jessica turned in her seat and grinned. "Miss Fyler, wasn't your first pet a T-Rex?"

The classroom laughed. Liz smiled, shook her head dramatically, and walked up to Alanna. "I see your class is well behaved."

"You should have seen them when we first started school."

The class giggled.

"I wanted to let you know a new student will be joining you next week. Romero Sanchez. The town council accepted the family's application to join our community. I met him this morning. He seems smart and well-behaved."

"He won't fit in with this group," called out Ginny from the front row. The class laughed.

"We look forward to having him." Alanna turned to her class. "Don't we?"

Being serious for once, the other students agreed.

"Thanks. I'll bring Romero in on Monday and introduce him."

"Sounds good."

Liz headed for the door, glancing over at the class. "Don't give Miss Daniels too much trouble. You wouldn't be here if it wasn't for her."

The students became quiet. Though they lovingly gave Alanna a hard time, each of them owed their lives to her.

The apocalypse began for Alanna with a nightmare. Her family had been trying to escape Manchester, New Hampshire, the day the zombie outbreak broke out in their city, getting stuck in gridlocked traffic on I-93. A horde of the living dead swarmed over the vehicles, ravaging drivers and passengers. As they approached her SUV, Alanna's mother turned around and tried freeing her baby brother from his car seat. She turned to Alanna and ordered, firm but lovingly, "Run. We'll catch up to you."

Alanna opened the door and rushed out, making it fifty feet down the highway before turning to check on her family. Her mother had freed her baby brother and started to run after Alanna when five zombies jumped her. Dad tried to pull them off but failed. Alanna watched as her parents were ravaged by the living dead. Four zombies went after her brother, ripping him apart, feeding on his arms and legs like they were chicken wings. Fear and desperation overwhelmed Alanna. She turned and raced to safety.

Other than the slaughter of her family, Alanna had little recollection of those first few days of the apocalypse. Somehow, she avoided the ravaging horde and made it to the safety of the nearby woods, running and walking for days, trying to avoid both the living and the living dead. Eventually, she came across a lone house located on a back road and decided to stay there and rest.

That was where she met Kevin and Jessica. The kids' parents had not returned from work and their babysitter had abandoned them. Alone and terrified, the kids let her in and asked Alanna to protect them. Though she was only eleven at the time, Alanna agreed. She could not leave them to die alone. Plus, saving them might ease the inner torment she struggled with after watching her own family get devoured.

Like everyone else, life over the next few years had been terrifying beyond anyone's darkest imagination. The three stayed at the home for a week until a zombie horde swarmed the neighborhood, forcing them to flee. Fortunately for Alanna and the kids, within a week they stumbled across a National Guard unit that had formed an organized retreat toward the Appalachian Mountains and took them in, picking up other survivors as well as other National Guard units and militia forces along the way. It took over a week to reach the range and over a month to set up defensive positions, but luck had been on their side. Using the elevation to their advantage, the group prevented the living dead from overwhelming them and survived long enough to join the effort to take back the country.

Since Alanna cared for Kevin and Jessica, she became the *de facto* guardian of any orphans taken in, despite her only being eleven. Agnes, a nurse who ran the makeshift hospital, confided to Alanna that she got the responsibility dumped on her since it freed up the adults for other tasks. Not that Alanna minded. She enjoyed being the babysitter for the children who had lost their parents. Having shared the same horrifying experiences, they became a close-knit group. Over time, Alanna convinced Agnes to let the older children help at the hospital, doing tasks they could handle and freeing up the medical staff to focus on priorities. It gave the kids a sense of belonging.

By the beginning of the first winter, Alanna had twenty-three children under her care. Five died during the harsh weather, and one three-year-old girl was bitten by a stray zombie that wandered into the compound one night. Alanna put the girl out of her misery after she turned, an action that, while necessary, still gave her anxiety-ridden dreams. Despite that, she kept the group alive and as happy as possible under the circumstances.

Once the campaign to clear the country of zombies had concluded, and the remaining living dead were isolated in cities, the group of orphans disbanded. Several of the older ones joined the forces assigned to surround the cities and keep the threat isolated. Agnes adopted two girls she had become close to at the hospital. The commander of the mountain retreat showed his appreciation for all Alanna had done by offering to transport her anywhere she wanted to settle. She asked to go back to New England since she was born and raised there. A week later, a helicopter flew her from the Appalachians to Nahant. The seven remaining orphans begged to stay with her. Alanna could not abandon them, so they joined her on the island. They were given their own home to live in and, because of her reputation for supporting the children, Mayor Wright asked her to run a class and teach the children the basics. She accepted without hesitation.

The seven orphans who joined Alanna now sat in her class. Kevin and Jessica, now ten and eleven. Norman, eight years old, had been on a camping trip with his parents at the time of the outbreak. His family had been attacked while making their way home, his parents and uncle not surviving the encounter. Myles was the same age as Alanna and rarely left her side. No one knew his backstory. He wandered into the mountain compound one night and was discovered by a guard on duty who took him to Alanna. Myles proved to be a good kid, did as he was told, and helped out as much as possible, but had not spoken a word since she took him in. Heather was seven. She could not recall the incident that led to her becoming an orphan, probably because she blocked the memories. A militia unit found her while on patrol, wandering along a back road, clutching a blood-soaked teddy bear. Heather still kept that teddy bear with her to this day. And Carissa, now twelve. At first, the girl had been defiant, causing Alanna nothing but trouble. One night, Alanna saw Carissa sitting outside, crying, and took the opportunity to talk with her. Carissa had been reluctant to speak but eventually told Alanna how she had enjoyed watching the zombies break into their house and eat her parents because her father had sexually abused her, and her mother allowed it. Carissa hid in her attic for a week until the zombies wandered away, then left the house to look for a better place to live, eventually being picked up by a patrol. She had struggled for years with the emotional conflict between being glad her parents died a violent death and the guilt over not mourning their loss. After that discussion, the two girls became friends.

The remaining three students in the classroom—Debbie, Sean, and Myeong-hwa—all had parents who had relocated to Nahant in recent months. Next week, Romero would join them.

"Alright, class. Who knows what an oral history is?"

Kevin raised his hand. "Isn't that when you read a history book out loud?"

"Good guess, but no. History books are written by men and women who tell stories about historical events. Oral history is when an average person talks or writes about their experiences."

"Crap," muttered Sean. "Another writing assignment."

Alanna suppressed a smile. "Yes, another writing assignment. But this one is important. It will let future generations know what we went through."

"Let me guess the topic," said Myeong-hwa good-naturedly. "The topic is 'what I did during the zombie apocalypse'."

"Correct."

Most of the class groaned.

"I could make the writing assignment about how awesome your teacher is."

"That would be even harder," joked Kevin.

The class chuckled.

Alanna went over to the cabinet and handed out writing paper and pens to the class. As she passed by Karen, the girl asked, "How long does it have to be?"

"As long as you want it, but I suggest writing down everything you can remember. Something like this will never happen again, so those who read this in the future need to know what we went through."

CHAPTER TWO

LIEUTENANT GARY BOSTWICK was woken by his telephone. Satellite connections had not yet been restored, so the ringing was that shrill, annoying clatter you heard only in old black and white movies. It startled Bostwick out of his slumber, the tone not as annoying as the fact that the only time he received a call was when something had gone wrong. He rolled over, sat up on the edge of the bed, and answered on the fourth ring.

"Yeah?" The lieutenant glanced over at the alarm clock, which read 4:23. "This had better be important."

"It's Corporal Simmons at the monitoring center. Sorry to wake you, lieutenant, but we have sensor reports of unusual activity in the Callahan Tunnel."

Bostwick yawned. "What type of unusual activity?"

"A large mass is moving through the tunnel toward East Boston."

"Describe large."

"The mass is covering both lanes and stretches for nearly a mile."

Bostwick stood and began to slide on his trousers with his free hand. "What do the monitors show?"

"Nothing. Whatever is down there must have knocked over the tripods and put them out of commission."

"Shit! Hang on." Bostwick laid the phone on the nightstand, zipped up his trousers, and secured the belt. The most likely scenario would be ZEDs—the zombie dead. But there would have to be hundreds of them to create a mass that size, and daily helicopter flyovers of the city and street patrols had seen no signs of the living dead, let alone a horde. As he slid on his socks and boots, the lieutenant wedged the phone between his shoulder and cheek. "Are any of the other monitors showing movement?"

"No, sir. Before calling you, I checked with the security posts around the perimeter. No one has spotted anything unusual."

"Good call. Keep an eye on that mass. I'll be there in a few minutes."

Hanging up the phone, Bostwick finished dressing, rushed out of his house, and climbed into his jeep. The trip from the barracks to the Logan Command Center would take only a few minutes.

The barracks, as the unit jokingly referred to them, were the abandoned residences on the island of Winthrop, directly across the sound from Logan International Airport. During the operation to isolate Boston and let the ZEDs wither away, a barrier of cargo containers had been erected between the terminal and the runways, trapping the ZEDs stuck inside the building. The containers were stacked three high on the outer row, two high in the center, and one high on the interior facing the city. The runways were used to bring in supplies and reinforcements and to hold the helicopters that made daily surveillance flights over Boston. The residences on Winthrop quartered the troops, with a pontoon bridge separating the two bodies of land. In the first few months after setting up, there were daily battles stopping the ZEDs that swarmed the barricades in search of food. Over time, as the fighting culled out the living dead, the conflicts decreased in intensity until only stragglers made their way to the barricade. For the past eight months, not a single ZED had been observed. It had been a peaceful and, thankfully, boring post.

Until tonight.

Parking in front of the metal shipping container that served as the monitoring station, Bostwick entered the structure, heading directly to Simmons' station.

"What's the current situation, corporal?"

"I've lost contact with the mass."

Bostwick rested his left hand on the desk and leaned over to study the monitor. "How?"

"Whatever caused the sensors to go off must have exited the tunnel."

"Which means they're now in East Boston."

"Correct, sir."

"Then switch on the cameras and let's see what it is."

Simmons hesitated a few seconds before responding. "We do not have cameras above ground."

"Why not?"

"The previous commander felt it would be too costly since we have a squadron of helicopters and drones to fly over the city. He only installed cameras and sensors in the Callahan and Sumner Tunnels and at some of the subway stations."

"So, what you're telling me is that we're blind."

"Yes, until we can get the choppers or drones airborne." Simmons glanced up at Bostwick. "Sorry, sir."

"It's not your fault. How many drone pilots are on duty?"

"None. There are three on call, but they're back in Winthrop. It'll take at least half an hour to get them here and get the drones airborne. The same with the chopper crews."

"Fuck." Bostwick contemplated his options. "Call the crews and get them over here pronto. I'll be back in a few minutes."

"Where are you going?"

"To check in with the guard posts on the barricade. Maybe they've seen something."

CORPORAL PALMER STOOD guard at his position in the center of the southern portion of the barricade directly across from

Logan terminal. Two others shared the shift with him. Privates Childs and Norris. Three more soldiers manned the northern section. Though, to be honest, six soldiers on duty seemed a bit overboard. No ZEDs had been sighted along this portion of the perimeter, or along any segment of the perimeter, in months. Not that Palmer was complaining. Life at the Logan Command Center was fucking boring, with nothing to do when not on duty except sit around, read, work out, or play video games. And since they only had three video games for the entire base, he had already played through them so many times that they had become boring. Being bored was preferable after almost two years of combat against the ZEDs.

A cool breeze blew in from the ocean, a welcome relief from the heat and humidity that hung over Boston like a wet towel. Thankfully, it came from the east. When it blew in from the west, it carried the stench of hundreds of thousands of decayed corpses that littered the city. In the first few weeks, he puked every shift. By now, he had become used to it, though he would never appreciate the stench from the city.

Footsteps approached from his left, the military boots clanging on the metal. Childs stepped up, holding a cigarette between his fingers, a bad habit that had become a luxury in this new world.

“Corporal, do you have a lighter? I left mine at the barracks.”

“I do if you have one for me.”

“Shit.” Childs gave Palmer his cigarette, then fished a package of Camels out of his pocket, taking one for himself. “You know how much I paid for these?”

“Like you have anything better to do with your money.” Palmer removed his lighter, flicked it on, and lit the two cigarettes.

“Any chance of me getting one?” asked Norris as he joined them.

“Fuck, man. I ain’t no convenience store.”

Palmer took a drag on the cigarette and handed it to Norris. "You can have mine. I've lost the taste for them."

"Thanks." Norris put it between his lips and inhaled, holding the smoke in for several seconds before blowing it out with a sigh of satisfaction. "It's been so long since I've had one—"

"Ten shun," blurted Palmer as Bostwick reached the top of the ladder and stepped onto the barricade. All three men snapped to attention, Childs and Norris trying to hide the cigarettes behind their backs.

"At ease. And enjoy the smokes."

Childs and Norris relaxed.

"The sensors detected a mass movement inside the Callahan Tunnel heading this way. Have you seen any unusual activity?"

"No, sir," said Palmer.

"What caused it?" asked Norris.

"No clue."

Palmer looked at his two shift mates and then back at the lieutenant. "ZEDs?"

Bostwick shrugged. "The drones and choppers would have spotted that many roaming the city."

"Equipment malfunction?" offered Childs.

Bostwick shrugged again. "That's what my money is on. I came up to see if you had seen anything unu—"

A strange noise emanated from the other side of the barricade, a combination of movement and squealing. All four men turned toward the sound. A mass moved around the southern end of the terminal and spread out, rapidly flowing across the tarmac.

"What the…?" Childs let the question die off.

Norris glanced over at the lieutenant. "Is it a tidal surge?"

"It's coming from inland and not the coast." Bostwick switched on the spotlight to his right and shone it on the mass.

A horde of rats swarmed across the tarmac. The pack stretched two hundred feet across, the center layered up to five rats high, the vermin scurrying over one another. The height thinned out along the edges, with several of the creatures leaving the pack to sniff something, then scurrying back. The rear of the pack had not yet come around the terminal.

Norris grabbed the binoculars from their mount and raised them to his eyes.

"Where did so many of them come from?" asked Palmer.

"The scout teams have been reporting for months that the rodent population has been increasing as they feed off the dead." Childs glanced at each of his crewmates, seeing if they agreed. "They must have come from Boston."

Norris lowered the binoculars, terror filling his eyes. "Those are not rats."

Palmer grabbed the binoculars and studied the swarm. "You gotta be fuckin' kidding."

"I'm not," said Norris. "Those are zombie rats."

"Give me those." Bostwick took the binoculars and trained them on the horde.

The pack was a grotesque mass of rot swarming along in a tidal wave of gore. Hundreds of thousands of living dead rodents in various stages of decay. Several limped along, limbs missing, propelled by the swarm. Others had their abdomens torn open, some with empty bodies, others with entrails hanging out and dragging behind them. Some had tattered and chewed flesh hanging off their bodies. All of them had maggots crawling across their rotted bodies, feasting on the dead flesh, sharing the food with a swarm of flies hovering over the pack. The only thing more disgusting than the sight of the living dead rats was the stomach-churning stench of decay emanating from the pack.

The apparent leader, a rat whose body was nearly four feet long from nose to tail, had half the skin ripped off its face, exposing the left side of its skull, the milky-white eye still in its socket. Upon noticing the soldiers atop the barricade, it turned toward them and squealed, an ungodly sound emanating from its rotted vocal cords. The entire pack squealed in unison and converged on the barricade.

Panic filled Palmer's voice. "We'll never kill that many rats."

"Don't worry," responded the lieutenant. "We're three containers high. They'll never get over the barricade."

The pack slammed into the first row of containers, their weight echoing off empty interiors. The swarm slowed, unable to move forward.

Bostwick glanced over at the others. "What did I tell you?"

"Sir?" Norris pointed toward the pack, his hand shaking.

The pack grew taller as more and more rodents piled on top of one another. In less than a minute, the horde spilled over into the first row of containers and rushed forward, forming beneath the second row. Soon, the mass reached the top of that row and swarmed forward, collecting at the third row beneath the soldiers.

"What are we going to do?" asked Palmer.

Bostwick knew they had only one option. "Get the fuck out of here."

Norris raced to the ladder and began descending, followed a second later by Childs. Bostwick grabbed Palmer by the arm. "Give me your weapon."

The corporal unslung the M14 Enhanced Battle Rifle and a pouch of spare ammo magazines, then handed them to Bostwick. "What for?"

"I'll hold them off and give you guys a chance to escape."

Palmer swung around and climbed down two rungs before stopping. "Good luck."

Bostwick flipped off the safety and stepped over to the other side of the container. The mass was inches from flowing over the top. He leaned over and fired, aiming for those closest to the rim. The bullets tore into the rats, ripping apart those supporting the climbing pack, creating a cloud of gore. Flies flew off the pack, many of them swarming around Bostwick's head, disrupting his aim. As the magazine ran empty, the mound collapsed, sending hundreds of the living dead vermin tumbling onto the container beneath it.

Bostwick switched out the empty magazine with a full one, cocked back the lever, and peered over the edge.

"Fuck."

The rats had formed two more mounds on either side of the one he had just taken down, both already within a foot of the rim. He aimed at the one on the left, using the same tactic as before, emptying an entire magazine and breaking apart the mound. Changing out the magazines, Bostwick turned to the right.

Rodents had already crested the top of the container and rushed toward him. Bostwick picked off the first eight before he ran out of ammunition. The horde grew larger, reaching more than a hundred. The lieutenant backed up as he attempted to switch out the magazines. Rodents swarmed over him. He tried to brush them off, but for each he knocked aside, three more took their place. Pain ran through his body as they bit off chunks of flesh and chewed their way into his muscles. One oversized rodent ran up his back, across his shoulders, and chomped into his right eye, rupturing the orb. Two had begun tearing their way into his intestines. Panic overcame Bostwick. He thrashed around in desperation until he toppled over the guardrail and plummeted to the runway thirty feet below, shattering his body and putting the lieutenant out of his misery.

NORRIS AND CHILDS reached the bottom of the ladder and backed onto the runway, waiting for Palmer. Norris looked up and yelled.

"Watch out!"

Palmer shifted his gaze upward as half a dozen rats flowed over the top. Four dropped to the ground. One bounced off his shoulder, ricocheted off the container, and fell to its death. The sixth landed on Palmer's shoulder. He screamed and slapped it off before it could bite, then jumped the last few feet to the ground. Norris and Childs ran over and helped him up.

"Are you okay?" asked Norris.

"Yeah." Palmer shook himself. "Thank god that mother—"

A scream of terror interrupted him, followed by the sickening smash of Bostwick crashing against the tarmac. The three men turned, too shocked to move. Those rodents on the lieutenant that survived raced off him and headed toward the fresh food. More flowed over the top of the container, joining the others.

Palmer glanced around, spotting an empty storage container twenty feet away with the doors open.

"We can hide in there."

The three dashed toward the safe haven.

Two rodents caught up with them and jumped onto Norris' leg, each taking a bite. Norris screamed and toppled onto the asphalt. Palmer ran over to his friend, removed his sidearm, and shot the two rats. Palmer lifted Norris and helped the wounded man to the container as Childs provided cover, falling back and picking off any rat that came close. Norris and Palmer reached the container and headed for the back.

"We're in," shouted Palmer.

Childs fired off the last rounds from his sidearm, futilely tossed the weapon at the swarm, and ran to join his friends. Once inside, he slammed shut the first door and reached for the second. Four rats rushed in as he closed it. A moment later, the pack reached the container, hitting the outside with such force that the impact echoed inside.

Three of the rodents headed for Norris and Palmer. The fourth hovered near Childs, who crushed it under his boot.

One went after Norris, biting him on the leg. Palmer yanked it off and flung it so hard against the wall that its head shattered, splattering the metal wall in blood and gore. The other two attacked Palmer, one crawling up his leg. He pulled it off, only to be bitten in the hand. Palmer dropped it to the floor and crushed it while the second raced up his back and bit him in the neck. He pulled it off and, while holding it, stepped on its head. Its squeals of fury ended when its skull exploded under his boot with a loud crack, its brains splattering across the floor.

With the threat gone, Childs put his ear against the door. As he listened, the squealing and scratching subsided. He heard the pack moving away from the container and across the runway.

"They're gone. We'll give them a few minutes, then find a way out—"

Moaning came from the other end of the container. An emptiness filled Childs' stomach as he slowly turned toward the noise, terrified at what he would find.

Norris and Palmer stood several feet away, their eyes milky white, their bodies slightly hunched over. His friends had passed on and joined the ranks of the living dead.

"Shit."

Looking up, the zombies' attention focused on Childs. Letting out a hungry cry, they attacked.

SIMMONS SAT IN front of the terminal with his headphones on, scanning the sensors for any sign of the unknown mass and monitoring the chatter between the helicopter crew and drone pilots on their way. He thought he heard a commotion outside but ignored it, writing it off as his imagination until the sound reached him a second time. Simmons removed his headphones as the noise intensified. It sounded like… gunfire. Placing the headphones on the counter, he went over to the door and opened it.

"What the hell is—"

Thousands of rats were dropping off the barricade like a waterfall and spreading out across the runway, the closest only ten feet away. The leader, a four-foot-long rodent with half its face eaten away, turned to him and squealed. As if on command, hundreds broke from the pack and raced toward the command center. Simmons realized he would not be able to close the door in time and made a suicidal decision, but one that needed to be made.

Simmons ran back to the console and grabbed the microphone.

"This is a flash alert to all units. I repeat, this is a flash—"

The warning devolved into an anguished cry as the rodents covered his body. Simmons slammed his back against the console, killing ten of the creatures. Not that it mattered. More of the zombie rats covered his body, chewing chunks out of his flesh and muscles. The pain became excruciating. Simmons removed his firearm from its holster and shot himself in the head. His body collapsed to the floor, providing a still warm meal for the hundreds of rodents that fed on his carcass.

MASTER SERGEANT HOPPER, in command of the helicopter unit, led the crews across the pontoon bridge, the drone pilots not far behind them.

"What the hell is so important that we had to be woken up so early?"

"This sucks big time."

"Maybe it's a drill. We haven't had one in months."

"At night? What the hell do they expect us to see in the dark?"

Hopper stopped short and spun around, causing the others to pile into each other. "Knock off the bitching. The command center picked up something massive moving through the Callahan Tunnel and had no idea what it was. We've been called to do our job, which is to fly over the city and see what it is. I don't want—"

Gunfire and screaming cut off the sergeant. Hopper spun

around, trying to figure out what was going on. His co-pilot came up alongside him and pointed ahead.

"I think we found that moving mass."

Hundreds of thousands of rats flowed across the runways a hundred feet away, a swarm of flies hovering above them, rapidly moving toward the unit. The lead rodent, a four-foot monstrosity, emitted an ungodly squeal. The pack increased speed, closing in on the humans.

Hopper spun around and issued a single command. "Run!"

The sergeant knew their chances of survival were non-existent. Within seconds, the rodents swarmed over the unit, twenty-two soldiers in total, dragging them to the ground and tearing into them, chewing through their skin and devouring their organs. Those that could not find space to feed continued ahead, crossing the pontoon bridge and converging on Winthrop.

Most of the other troops were outside, heading to the mess hall for morning chow, only to be caught off guard. Having left their weapons in their quarters, they had no chance of fighting back. Scores of men and women died within minutes, devoured by the pack. The few lucky survivors raced back to their quarters and locked themselves in, delaying the inevitable. Knowing food existed inside, the rodents chewed through the front doors and invaded the premises, hunting down and killing their prey. Those who had not been caught out in the open emerged from their homes to see what was going on, only to fall victim to the incessant rodents. Within twenty minutes, every living person within the compound had been devoured, leaving behind skeletons with only bits of flesh on them.

When no more food was available, the leader squealed several times, calling back its living dead minions. Once they had gathered, the leader led the pack north, heading toward Revere.

CHAPTER THREE

NATE PHILLIPS ENJOYED visiting Barterville. Not only did it give him a chance to socialize, but it also reminded him of his old job as an Amazon delivery driver before the zompoc. Only now, he didn't have a set route to follow and did not have to take photos of his deliveries. He spent his time commuting from one compound to another, gathering their wish lists and the items they wanted to trade, then searching for those items. It was much more fun than fighting the ZEDs for three years.

Having spent the last two hours strolling through the various stalls, Nate had yet to find anything on the list, which bummed him out. He enjoyed watching the smiles on the residents' faces, especially the children, when they received an item they had asked for. Well, maybe next time.

A howl echoed through Barterville. It came from Fred, his Beagle. The two met five months ago while Nate was taking a break along the coast, having lunch. The dog, scared and emaciated, cautiously approached, begging to get something to eat. Nate shared his sandwich. By the third bite, the dog sat beside him, his front paws on Nate's leg and his tail wagging furiously. He adopted the dog, or more appropriately, the dog adopted him. He named the dog Fred after a co-worker who always forgot to bring his lunch. Fred now served as his alarm, staying with the pickup and barking whenever a customer showed up.

Nate made his way back to the pickup, a 1974 Chevrolet K20. Fred sat in the truck bed, his front paws on the rim, searching for his owner. At the sight of Nate, his tail began to wag. Fred barked excitedly.

A young woman stood by the pickup, scratching Fred's back. She stood slightly above average. Judging by her appearance, he guessed she was in her late teens. He remembered her because she was attractive. He vaguely recalled her name but could not remember where he had seen the woman before.

"Hello, Alina."

She turned to him and smiled. "It's Alanna."

"Sorry." He blushed from embarrassment. "How can I help you?"

"I run the school. I'm trying to create a feeling of community among my kids and wondered if you had any clothes with the same logo on them."

"You mean the school's logo?"

"Any logo. It could be for another school, a sports team, anything. So long as it has the same design to unite the class."

"I don't have anything like that in stock."

Alanna frowned with disappointment. "Thanks anyway."

The young woman turned to leave when Nate suddenly remembered something. "Wait a second."

Alanna spun around, an expression of hope on her face. "Yes."

"There's a compound on Revere Beach that came across a bunch of t-shirts for a restaurant near their housing. It's called Kelley's Roast Beef. Will that do?"

"Yes," she said excitedly.

"How many do you need?"

"As many as you can get me." The smile drained from Alanna's face. "What will they want in trade?"

"Nothing."

"Are you serious?"

Nate nodded. "I've been bartering with them for a while now. We're friends. Once I tell them why you want the shirts,

I'm sure they'll donate them."

"I don't know how to thank you."

"Find some treats for Fred, and we'll be even."

The dog barked in agreement. Alanna scratched behind his ears.

"How long do you think it'll take to get them?"

"I plan on coming back in two days. I'll swing by the Revere compound on my way home tonight and pick them up for you. How does that sound?"

"It's perfect. The kids will be so excited. Thanks again." Alanna raced back to the school to share the good news.

Nate turned to the pickup, pulled Fred close, and kissed the top of his head. "Looks like we did our good deed for the day."

Fred wagged his tail in agreement.

CHAPTER FOUR

COLONEL KEVIN WHITAKER sat behind the office desk performing his daily routine—reading and initialing reports, approving supply requisitions, and trying not to doze off.

Three months ago, Lieutenant General McKinnon of the Massachusetts Zombie Combat Command offered him the position as commander of the Massachusetts Combat Aviation Brigade (MCAB) headquartered in Salem. Whitaker accepted because he figured it would be less stressful than being on the front lines for two years. After participating in the Battle for the Appalachians and the nearly disastrous Battle of Charlestown, and being involved in Operation Freedom Trail, which contained the ZEDs in Boston, the idea of having a desk job seemed a welcome relief.

He never expected the assignment to be so boring.

MCAB was established to assist in any ZED cleanup operations that broke out in Massachusetts. The command headquarters had been set up at Salem State University for two reasons. First, it was the ideal location between the state's ZCZs (ZED Containment Zones). Second, the location provided the necessary facilities. The dorms were used as living quarters, the college classrooms as offices, and the parking lots as helicopter landing zones. By the time Whitaker took over, all the ZEDs had either been killed or contained, so their mission devolved into assisting in supply runs and the occasional medical evac to local hospitals.

His telephone rang. He picked it up. "Colonel Whitaker speaking."

"Colonel, it's Lieutenant Reynolds from the Comm Center. We just received a request to send a chopper to check with a Boston ZCZ station. The station sent a message earlier in the morning that was garbled and has not responded for several hours."

"Can't they send a ground unit?"

"They could, but the station is isolated at Logan Airport. They would have to drive around the entire containment zone to check on them. It would be quicker to send in a chopper."

At first, Whitaker wanted Reynolds to tell the Boston ZCZ commander to get off his ass and do his job. However, considering how bored his pilots were, this would at least provide a diversion.

"Tell them a chopper will be there within the hour. Who has the least flight time in the group?"

"Captain Denning."

"Assign it to him."

"Her, sir. It's Captain Eileen Denning."

"No matter. It'll add to her flight time."

"Roger that, colonel." The line went dead.

Whitaker checked the time. A little before four o'clock. Screw it. He would hit the gym, grab dinner, then head to the officer's club.

CHAPTER FIVE

CAROL SAT ON the bench beneath the bandstand on Revere Beach, nursing a cup of hot coffee as she stared out over the ocean. She would have preferred an iced coffee, but civilization had not come back that far to make ice a priority. Not that it really mattered. She sat here for the view, not the drink.

She had been born and raised in Revere, and the beach had been a major part of her life. Her parents took Carol and her two brothers here every weekend during the summer for a day of swimming topped off with dinner at Kelley's Roast Beef. As she got older, the girls came here every Friday night to chat and gossip about the teachers and students they disliked. She also lost her virginity here, although that memory always got pushed to the back of her mind because her boyfriend had no clue how to please a woman. Coming back to Revere after the apocalypse gave her some closure.

Though not much.

Carol had been attending college at Syracuse University, studying psychology, and was in the middle of her senior year when the outbreak occurred. She had read numerous times about PTSD but only came to understand its significance after the zombies had finally been eliminated. The memories flooded into her consciousness despite all attempts to bury them. Watching her best friend, Morgana, being bitten and agonizingly becoming one of the living dead, then being forced to kill her. Being gang raped by a group of raiders. And, once the vaccine was retrieved from Boston and she joined the defense forces taking back the country, the countless battles and horrors she had endured fighting zombies. When the war ended, she came back to Revere hoping to rebuild her shattered life, only to find her family home burned out and no trace of her parents or brothers. She assumed they had joined the ranks of the living dead and were now buried in a mass grave somewhere.

Thankfully, she stumbled across a group of survivors trying to revitalize the city. They had established a residence in an old nursing home across the street from Kelley's. It offered the ideal arrangement: separate bedrooms and baths with communal living and dining areas. Carol joined the team cleaning out the condo and apartment complexes further south along the beach, preparing them for permanent use. In the past month, they had been able to prepare only two floors for newcomers, but at least it gave Carol a sense of doing something to help return society to normal.

Or the new normal they would have to live with.

"Hey, gorgeous."

Carol glanced over her shoulder. James stood behind her, his hands nervously wedged into his pockets. He was the one who welcomed her into the new community when she first arrived. They became friends quickly. However, James liked her as more than a friend, although he had yet to ask her out. To be honest, Carol crushed on James the first time she saw him, but was fighting too many psychological demons to take him to bed.

"What's up, handsome?"

"I saw you sitting here and thought you might want company." James suddenly grew nervous. "But if you'd rather be alone—"

Carol smiled warmly and patted the bench. "I'd love for you to join me."

James quickly circled the bench and sat down beside Carol.

She noticed he turned slightly toward her, his arm resting on the back of the bench near her shoulder. She shifted her body to complete the circle.

"What are you thinking about?" he asked.

"Nothing in particular. Just relaxing and enjoying the view." Carol sighed contentedly. "After so many years of avoiding and fighting zombies, sometimes it's hard to chill and enjoy life."

"I know. Cleaning out those apartments brings back horrible memories."

"Right now, I want to focus on the view. And the company."

James smiled. Carol didn't object when he slid closer to her.

MADDY STOOD IN front of the door to apartment 311. The team was three-quarters of the way through preparing the third floor for occupancy.

Cleaning out the building had been disgusting. It was a nightmare of death, with hundreds of mummified corpses that had to be removed and disposed of. Hallways and apartments were covered in dried blood and gore, staining the carpets and walls, and much of the furniture was either broken or covered in gore. After so many years of being closed up, stench permeated every inch of the building. The teams had to dispose of the corpses, clean up the mess, remove the useless stuff to a large burn pit out back, and keep all the windows open to air out the place. Then they filled the apartments with good furniture from those on the upper floors. All but two of the units on the first and second floors were ready for occupancy. Once finished, families from further inland could start moving in.

"It's getting late. Maybe we should wait until tomorrow to open this one up," suggested Stephen, her boyfriend.

"I don't intend to do any cleaning. I just want to get an idea what needs to be done tomorrow."

"Fair enough." Stephen pulled the lock-picking kit from his backpack and knelt in front of the door. He removed the tools from their mounts, inserted the tension wrench into the bottom of the keyhole and the curved hook into the top, and began picking. It took only seven seconds for him to unlock the door.

"You're getting good at this."

"I learned how to do this during the outbreak. It helped me find supplies to stay alive." He replaced the tools in the case and then stood. "Ready?"

Maddy raised the Mossberg shotgun into the high-ready position. "Let's do this."

Stephen banged on the door three times. No response came from inside the apartment. He grabbed the knob, turned it to the right, and pushed. The door moved only a few inches, shoving something heavy behind it. No zombies attacked. An intense stench of decay overwhelmed them. Stephen gagged.

"Pussy." Maddy refused to admit she almost puked.

"I'll never get used to the smell of the dead." Stephen stuck his head inside, expecting to find a dead body. Instead, someone had shoved a couch against the door. He pushed the door again, moving the blockade enough for him to squeeze past. "Hello."

When nothing responded, he entered and pulled the couch away from the door. Maddy slid past him, the shotgun still in the high-ready position. They moved across the living room and opened the sliding glass doors leading to the patio. The smell of fresh air dissipated some of the horrible odor.

Stephen walked around the room, checking out the furniture. "Everything here is in good shape. All we need to do is get the smell out of it."

"That's good." Maddy lowered the shotgun. "Let's check out the kitchen."

To their surprise, the kitchen was also in good shape. Stephen checked the cabinets.

"That's odd."

"What?"

He opened all the doors, revealing supplies of canned goods and pasta.

"What about the fridge?"

Stephen opened the refrigerator door, only to be greeted by the stench of rotted food.

"Gross," said Maddy.

Stephen laughed. "And I'm the pussy?"

She smiled and gave him the middle finger. "We'll clean it out tomorrow."

They maneuvered into the hallway. The closet to their right contained clothes in good condition.

Stephen nodded. "Once we wash these, we can trade them at Barterville."

Moving down to the next door on the right, Stephen knocked. When nothing responded, he opened the door and stepped inside. Maddy followed. One side contained a guest bed that had not been used in years. The rest of the room had been converted into a sewing area, with a Singer machine on a wooden table.

"Awesome," said Maddy. "Now we can make and repair our clothes."

Moving back into the hall, they stepped up to the only door on the left. The stench came from this room. Maddy raised her shotgun into the high-ready position. Stephen withdrew the Glock 19 from his holster.

"Ready?"

Maddy nodded.

Holding the semi-automatic pistol in his right hand, ready to fire, he used his left to open the door.

The odor of rotted flesh flowed out of the room like a tidal wave. Stephen turned and puked in the hallway. Maddy moved into the room, swinging her shotgun from left to right. There were no zombies.

The stench came from an old lady who had passed away peacefully in her bed. The corpse had rotted away and mummified after being trapped in a space without flowing air. Seven smaller skeletons surrounded her on the stained mattress. Maddy moved closer. They used to be cats. She grinned at the cliché of a crazy old cat lady, except these furry little bastards had fed off her body before they died. She felt sad for the pets. They reminded her of the four cats and the Pug she lost during the downfall of Washington.

Stephen entered the room, wiping his hand across his mouth. "Sorry."

"No problem. But you're cleaning it up."

"Fair enough." He looked over at the bed and bent over to vomit again.

Moving over to the window, Maddy pulled the curtains aside and lifted the pane to air out the room. They would give the old lady and her cats a proper burial tomorrow. Then everything in the room would be taken to the burn pit. It would be a long time before this apartment became livable.

"Let's get out of here and go back to the quarters. Supper should be ready soon."

Stephen grimaced. "I doubt I'll be able to keep anything down."

Maddy gave him a side hug. "You'll be fine."

Leaving the apartment, Stephen closed the door behind them. The door to room 312 remained open. Maddy stuck her head in.

"Are you guys done yet?"

"Almost," Jennifer called out. "Once Cheryl and I finish the kitchen, this place will be ready for occupancy. We'll meet you there soon."

"Sounds good."

Maddy and Stephen took the stairs down to the lobby, then exited into the driveway. She took Stephen's hand and smiled flirtatiously. "After dinner, I'll take your mind off of today."

Usually, Stephen would respond by grabbing her butt. Instead, he stared off to his right.

"Is everything okay?"

Stephen ignored her, muttering, "What the hell…."

Maddy followed his gaze. A black mass covering the road and stretching back as far as they could see flowed toward them. At first, she thought it was a tidal surge until she realized it came from along the road rather than the beach. And tidal surges were not covered in fur and flies. A few seconds later, a familiar and overpowering reek reached them, one both knew all too well—rotten flesh. Even from this distance, they could hear squeals, but not the squeals of normal vermin. Their cries had a familiar, tormented sound, similar to those that emanated from the living dead. The sudden and terrifying realization struck them.

"Are those what I think they are?" asked Stephen.

"Yes. Fucking zombie rats."

A decayed rat nearly four feet in length stood on its hind legs and emitted an anguished squeal. A massive segment of the pack turned left and headed toward the apartment building.

Stephen spun Maddy around and pushed her toward the nursing home. "Run!"

Maddy ran as if her life depended on it. Which it did. Stephen paused long enough to shout into the lobby.

"Cheryl, Jennifer. Lock yourselves in and stay quiet."

Seconds after he raced off, thousands of rats flooded the lobby and made their way upstairs.

CHERYL STOPPED CLEANING the stove and glanced over at the window. "Did you hear someone yelling?"

"No." Jennifer finished stuffing dirty paper towels into the trash bag and then headed to the living room balcony. "But something is going on outside."

Jennifer opened the sliding glass door, and both women stepped out. Cheryl gripped the handrail, her expression frozen in terror. Jennifer stared dumbfounded as the swarm of rats flowed around the building, with thousands rushing into the lobby.

Jennifer headed for the living room, pausing when she noticed Cheryl had not followed. The woman clasped the handrail so tightly her knuckles turned white.

"What are you waiting for?"

Cheryl did not budge.

Jennifer stepped over to her friend. "Come on."

Cheryl remained frozen. Jennifer pried the woman's hands off the guardrail, spun her around, and slapped her across the face. The blow brought Cheryl out of her stupor.

"We have to get out of here while we have the chance."

Both women ran out of the apartment and headed for the stairwell. The door was wedged open to air out the corridor. Jennifer stepped out onto the landing and paused, stretching out her arm to stop Cheryl.

"What's wrong? I thought we had to—" She heard the noise below.

Thousands of zombie rats swarmed up the stairs, already having reached the second-floor landing. Upon smelling their prey, they emitted a ghastly squeal and increased speed.

Jennifer shoved Cheryl into the corridor. "Get back to the apartment."

The two women ran for twenty feet when Jennifer spun around and headed back to the stairwell. If she removed the wedge and closed the metal fire door, it might delay the rats long enough for them to devise an escape plan.

Jennifer was five feet from the door when the first rat reached the landing and headed toward her. She froze. A second later, dozens more came through the doorway. Turning around, Jennifer sprinted down the corridor, glancing over her shoulder. She had enough distance between herself and the swarm so she should—

The slamming of a door and the click of a lock sent a chill down Jennifer's spine. Cheryl locked her out. Reaching the apartment, she pounded on the door.

"I'm fine. Open up."

"No." Cheryl's voice quivered on the other side. "I'm scared."

"Open the fucking door before I'm eaten a—"

A rat ran up Jennifer's leg and sank its teeth into her thigh, the sharp incisors cutting through her jeans and digging into flesh. She screamed and ripped it off, tearing off a large chunk of skin and muscle. Before she could throw it, more rats attacked. A few at first, then dozens, until finally they covered Jennifer, knocking her to the floor. She rolled across the carpet, trying to dislodge them, but to no avail. The pack rapidly stripped away her flesh and muscles, burrowing into her organs. One rodent bit through her right lid, rupturing the eye underneath. Jennifer screamed. When she did, a rat forced its way into her throat and fed off her tongue. A second chewed its way through her cheek. A third pushed past the first rat and made its way into her esophagus, chewing away at the tissue.

Jennifer lost her sanity seconds before she passed out from the pain, no longer experiencing the agony of being eaten alive by the living dead vermin.

Inside the apartment, Cheryl backed away from the door, the terror overwhelming her as Jennifer's anguished cries took on a muffled, maniacal tone, then ceased altogether. The squeals of the rodents continued. Then another sound echoed through the room, one more terrifying—teeth chewing away at the wooden door.

Not noticing the hassock behind her, Cheryl tripped over it, slamming onto the floor with such force that it momentarily stunned her. By the time her senses returned, the wood on the interior of the door began to crack. Standing up, she ran toward the balcony and stepped out.

A loud crack caught her attention. Cheryl turned to see a zombie rat push its decayed head through the door. The left side of its head had been eaten away, exposing its skull. The rat smelled its prey and screeched, then frantically shoved against the chewed hole. The opening grew larger. With a final shove, the vermin created a breach. Rats poured into the apartment and rushed for the balcony.

Cheryl backed up against the guardrail, screaming frantically and begging the rats to stop. Within seconds, they swarmed over her, knocking her off balance. She tumbled over the guardrail, the vermin consuming her as she plummeted through the air. Cheryl slammed into the pavement, breaking her neck and ending her misery.

JAMES GAZED INTO Carol's eyes and placed his hand on her shoulder. "I know this sounds weird. We haven't known each other that long."

"We've been working together for three months," she responded with a flirtatious smile.

"Fair enough. I was wondering if—"

A scream from farther down the beach cut off the conversation. Carol and James stood and moved onto the sidewalk. Carol gasped, the many nightmares from the past five years flooding back into her memory.

Several hundred feet away, thousands of rats moved toward them, covering the beach and road.

The scream had come from Maddy. Maddy and Stephen rushed down the road, the latter fifteen feet to the rear. The pack closed in.

"Get inside!" Stephen screamed, waving for the others to find safety. "There's thousands of…."

Stephen stumbled. He struggled to regain his footing, instead crashing onto the asphalt. Within seconds, rodents engulfed him. Their squealing grew more intense, second only to Stephen's agonized cries as they ripped into him, hundreds of tiny mouths devouring his flesh. The rest swarmed around him and continued ahead.

Maddy stopped and spun around, her last image of Stephen being his reaching out to her from under the pile of rats. She stood, stunned, uncertain what to do. The hesitation cost Maddy her life. One rat hurled itself at the woman, landing on her abdomen, biting through the shirt and into her skin. Maddy tore it off and tossed it aside. A second later, the pack struck, knocking her to the ground. Maddy's screams were drowned out as rats swarmed over her, burying her under dead flesh and fur.

The remainder of the pack headed for Carol and James.

Carol moved toward them.

James grabbed her arm. "What are you doing?"

"We have to help Maddy."

"It's too late for that. We need to get to safety before we're next."

They ran across the street to the nursing home.

As they approached the entrance, Kim opened the glass door and stepped out.

"What's all the…." Her eyes went wide upon seeing the rats. "What the fuck?"

Carol reached the steps first and shoved Kim back inside. James followed, stopping to lock the door. All three moved to the far end of the lobby, their attention focusing on the entrance.

The first rats slammed into the double glass doors, generating an ominous thud. They climbed on top of one another, slowly blocking the view until a sea of dead flesh and blood-matted fur covered the glass.

"D-do you think it'll hold?" asked Kim.

"It better," James replied. "If not, we're screwed."

He reached down and took Carol's hand in his own.

Carol gasped as cracks formed on the panes, rapidly extending like a spider web. Seconds later, the panes shattered, throwing shards of glass across the floor. The living dead swarmed into the lobby.

Kim panicked and headed for the office behind the front desk. Maneuvering around the counter slowed her. Several hundred rats crashed into her as she swung open the door, propelling her into the office. The screams of her death throes echoed across the first floor.

James pulled Carol down the corridor and pushed her into the first room, closing the door behind him. Scores of rats thudded against the door. James rushed over to the dresser.

"Help me move this."

They pushed it across the room and tipped the piece of furniture on its side, shoving it against the door. The pack had already begun chewing through the wood.

"That's not going to stop them," said Carol, fear cracking her voice.

"It'll slow them down. Follow me."

They raced across the room, pausing by the window. James glanced out and muttered a single word.

"Fuck."

The pack surrounded the building, blocking their escape.

"What now?" asked Carol.

James did not respond. They both knew the answer.

James led her to the single bed and laid down, patting the mattress beside him. Carol slid in beside James. He wrapped his arms around her, offering what little comfort he could. She clutched his arm tightly and sobbed.

The sounds of wood being shredded mixed with frantic squeals. James kept his eyes on the door, hoping their end would be quick. He noticed the dresser shake. The rats must have eaten their way through the door. The dresser shook again, this time moving half an inch. James held Carol tight and whispered in her ear.

"Don't worry, hon. It'll be over soon."

The dresser moved several inches, allowing the living dead to rush into the room. James braced himself for death, and Carol cried as the horde swarmed over the bed and began feeding.

NATE CRUISED ALONG the beach road, his window rolled down so he could enjoy the sea breeze. Reaching over, he scratched Fred behind his ears. The dog's wagging tail slapped against the leather seat.

"You're a good boy."

An unpleasant odor wafted through the cab. At first, Nate ignored it, writing it off as seaweed washing up on the sand. Only this did not have the usual briny smell of the ocean. It possessed an odor he had encountered too many times over the past few years.

A minute later, as Nate approached the Revere compound, he jammed his foot on the brake pedal. The pickup screeched to a stop. Fred lost his balance and tumbled onto the floor, then jumped back into his seat. Nate leaned forward, bracing his arms on the steering wheel, not able to believe what he witnessed.

"Jesus H. Christ on a fucking bicycle."

Rats covered the beach, more than he could imagine. The pack stretched as far as he could see. Off to the right, rats poured into the nursing home that the compound used as its living quarters. Even more terrifying, he could not spot a single human.

Upon sensing more food, the flood of vermin rushed toward the pickup.

"Hang on, boy."

Nate executed a three-point turn and accelerated the way

from which he had just come. Glancing into his rearview mirror, he saw the pack following him. Nate increased speed, putting as much distance as possible between him and the rats.

The dog growled and barked at the rear window.

"Come on, boy. We have to warn Nahant."

CHAPTER SIX

"WHAT'S OUR MISSION again, ma'am?" asked Master Sergeant Libby through the Huey's intercom.

Captain Eileen Denning kept her gaze fixed in front of them. "MCAB reported that one of the guard positions at the Boston ZCZ hasn't reported in for several hours and asked us to check it out."

"Why don't them lazy assholes do it themselves?"

"It's the station located at Logan Airport. It's isolated and would take them over an hour to get there."

"So, we have to do their work for them?"

"Relax." The co-pilot, First Lieutenant Plati, turned in his seat. "We were scheduled to do a flyover of the city anyway. It'll give you a chance to see your hometown."

"No thanks. It breaks my Italian heart to see what East Boston has become."

Denning agreed. Though from Louisiana, she had visited Boston a few years before the outbreak and fell in love with the city. Its vibrancy and nightlife reminded her of New Orleans. Especially Quincy Market, less than a mile from the harbor, which housed some of the best eateries in the state. She ate there every night, trying out a new restaurant each time, one night even picking up a waiter. The next time Denning returned to Boston was after the outbreak when assigned to do flyovers of the ZCZ. Her first mission took her by Quincy Market, the once beautiful area she remembered so fondly, now a carnage of decayed corpses and ZEDs.

Plati and Libby raised their binoculars, scanning the city along the starboard and port flanks, respectively, as Denning flew the Huey along Route 1 South. The chopper flew past the Mystic River Bridge, where a span on both the upper and lower decks had been blown off in a futile attempt to prevent the spread of the outbreak. Off to the left was the Charlestown Naval Shipyard. The *U.S.S. Constitution*, America's oldest warship, still sat at the dock. However, after five years of neglect, it appeared more like a ghost vessel from a horror movie than the grand representation of American history it once was.

When Route 1 merged with I-93 South, Denning veered the helicopter to the left and flew over the city. The Hancock Building and the Prudential Tower still dominated the skyline but were no longer the elegant buildings made famous in photographs. Most of the windows in the Hancock Building had been shattered, the shards covering the streets and reflecting sunlight. The Prudential was a burnt-out hulk from the fifth floor up, the building having become engulfed in flames on the first day of the outbreak, with no one available to put it out. Local witnesses claimed it burned for three days.

Beneath them, Boston was a nightmare. Hundreds of abandoned vehicles lined the streets, their numbers out-matched only by the tens of thousands of skeletons littering the city, those who had never made it out alive, and the corpses of the ZEDs that collapsed and rotted away from lack of food. She did not envy the clean-up crews who would have to remove all the bodies when… if… the government decided to reclaim the city.

Denning continued south until they reached Quincy, then veered left again and flew past the JFK Library, the memorial to the 35th President, now a ransacked hulk. Ahead sat Castle Island with the infamous Fort Castle, a relic of the American Revolution and one of the few positive events of the ZED outbreak. More than two hundred civilians barricaded themselves inside, surviving for more than a week as scores of the living dead swarmed the exterior walls. A Coast Guard helicopter discovered them while doing a final search of the area for survivors before abandoning Boston for good, and called in every available chopper in the vicinity to extract the civilians. Everyone in the fort survived.

Denning directed the helicopter toward Logan Airport.

"Libby, do you see anything?" she asked.

The master sergeant shook his head. "No one's manning the guard posts. I don't see any move…. Wait a minute."

"What is it?"

"There's a horde of rats on this side of the wall. Hundreds of them. But no signs…. Shit, fly closer and drop your altitude."

"Do you want me to land?"

"Hell no. Those rats look…. Jesus fucking Christ."

Denning was about to question Libby about what he saw, then paused, finally noticing the carnage for herself. Spread out among the scurrying rodents were several dozen bodies, their uniforms tattered and their bodies stripped clean of flesh, muscles, and organs.

Denning swallowed the bile rising in her throat. "Are those the guards?"

"It'd explain why no one's heard from them. We should…. Wait a minute. I see movement on the other side of the wall."

Denning flew the Huey to the left, crossing to the interior side of the container wall. Thousands of rats swarmed around the tarmac and terminal. On spotting the helicopter, they raced toward it, piling on top of one another to reach the food source, their squeals of hunger louder than the thumping of the engine.

"I've never seen rats act like that," said Denning.

"That's because they're zombie rats, just like the ZEDs."

"Are you sure?"

"Look for yourself." Libby reached around the pilot's seat and handed the binoculars to Denning. When she focused her gaze on the rodents, she realized, to her horror, that Libby was correct. Decayed bodies. Missing tails and legs. Skin chewed away, exposing skeletons and rotting organs. And a massive swarm of flies hovering over the pack. She had seen this more times than she cared to imagine during the outbreak among humans. Only then, it was fairly easy to take down a ZED with a headshot. How the fuck do you kill thousands of zombie rats?

"Plati, take pictures so we can confirm this with command. Then we'll go back to base and report this."

"Wait a minute." Plati tapped Denning on the shoulder and pointed toward Winthrop. "We need to check out the housing compound. Something's not right."

After Plati took photos of the guard post, Denning swung the Huey to the right, crossing the runways and passing over the bridge. They all spotted the carnage at the same time. Plati summed it up best when he muttered, "Jesus fucking Christ."

It looked the same as back at the wall, except rather than a dozen bodies, there were more than a hundred, stripped clean of any living tissue, the blood-stained pavement a grotesque backdrop to the skeletons. As with the rest of the compound, scores of ZED rats scavenged the neighborhood in search of food that had not already been stripped clean. Plati took photos of the carnage.

"Where are the rest of them?" asked Libby.

Denning turned her head to the right. "The rest of who?"

"The rats. There's no way those down there could have done that much damage in less than twenty-four hours."

Denning had not considered that.

"Keep scanning the flanks. We need to know where the horde went."

Glancing ahead, she decided to follow the main road through the peninsula, keeping the Huey at rooftop level. For several miles, they came across nothing unusual, just the same deserted and run-down neighborhoods that dominated the nation. She was about to give up and turn toward Salem when

Plati called out.

"Off to the right. About halfway down Revere Beach. I think I found them."

Denning maneuvered the Huey along the beach. It took only a second for her to spot the pack, though the word was an understatement. Hundreds of thousands of ZED rats overran a condominium complex and a two-story structure farther down, with even more stampeding down the road, a flood of decayed flesh and fur flowing toward the far end of the beach.

"I thought I'd seen the worst during the ZED war," said Libby from the rear of the chopper. "But this… this is a friggin' nightmare."

Denning pushed the horror from her mind and focused on operational necessities. "If they keep heading in this direction, they'll eventually reach Salem. Are there any settlements between the base and the rats?"

Plati finished taking photos and checked the chart. "No, ma'am."

"That's a relief."

Libby tapped the pilot on the shoulder and pointed to the right. "Isn't there a settlement over there?"

Denning glanced over at Nahant. "Shit."

Plati checked the chart again. "If the horde keeps going straight, Nahant should be safe."

"Better safe than sorry." Denning turned the Huey and headed back to Salem. "Contact base and warn them what's going on. And have them inform Nahant what's on its way."

CHAPTER SEVEN

"HOW MUCH IS this?" asked Sadie as she lifted the item off the table.

Brad frowned. "*What* is it?"

She glanced over at her lover, surprise in her eyes. "It's a porcelain mermaid."

"Why do you need that?"

"I don't." Sadie's tone developed an edge. "I *want* it."

He backed down.

"We're past trying to survive," replied Cerone, the vendor. "Now we're rebuilding society, one town and one memory at a time."

"You're right." Brad turned to Sadie. "Let me get it for you." He glanced over at Cerone. "What will you take for it?"

Cerone grinned and attempted to bail out Brad. "As long as the lovely young lady forgives you, it's free."

"Are you sure?" she asked.

Cerone nodded and handed the statue to Sadie, who placed it in her palms and marveled at it.

"It's awesome," she said, then leaned over and kissed Brad. "Just like you."

Brad held Sadie close and hugged her, glancing to his left and mouthing "thank you" to the vendor.

The couple continued walking along Barterville, checking out the various tables, when a young voice came from behind them.

"Hello, Miss Cummings."

Sadie turned around as Alanna raced up. "Please, call me Sadie."

"Okay." Alanna grinned. "How are you? I haven't seen you in a while."

"I'm fine. I've been busy. What are you doing here?"

"I was chatting earlier with Nate. He promised to pick up some t-shirts with identical logos so the kids can have uniforms." Alanna used finger quotes when saying uniforms.

As if on cue, Nate's pickup raced into the rotary at the end of the causeway, the engine revving loudly. Rather than pull into the side of the causeway where Barterville was, he swerved into the lanes on the opposite side of the divider and drove over one hundred miles per hour toward the island.

Alanna switched her gaze between Brad and Sadie. "What the hell was that about?"

"It can't be good," he said.

Eight minutes later, the bells of Saint Thomas Aquinas Church began ringing, startling everyone at Barterville.

"What's going on?" asked Cerone.

"It's okay," Sadie answered in a calm voice. "The sirens are used to call emergency town meetings."

Brad tapped Cerone on the shoulder. "I wouldn't worry about it. But I'd pack up and be ready to roll if I were you. And warn the other vendors to do the same."

"Thanks."

Brad, Sadie, Alanna, and the other Nahant residents headed to the town hall.

ETHAN STOOD IN front of the elevated altar, studying the faces of those attending the emergency meeting. Everyone chatted amongst themselves, trying to figure out what was going on, the noise unusually loud as everyone presented their own theory. Their expressions ranged from concern to fear, with a few bordering on panic. Not that he blamed them. This was the first time anyone had called such a gathering since resettling Nahant. The locals knew the ringing of the church bells signaled something bad must be going down.

None of them had any idea how dangerous the situation had become.

Ethan waited several minutes after the last person arrived, assuming no more were coming.

Melissa, his secretary, stepped up beside him and whispered, "I think everyone is here. Good luck."

Taking a few steps forward, Ethan raised his hands and called out to get the crowd's attention.

"Excuse me. I'd like to call this meeting to order."

Half the group quieted down and focused their attention on Ethan, while the other half still chatted amongst themselves. Melissa stepped forward.

"Hey! Listen up!"

The room went silent. She glanced over at Ethan and nodded. Ethan took a deep breath and slowly exhaled.

"We have a crisis developing and have to decide how to deal with it."

"What type of crisis?" asked Sadie.

Nate moved up beside Ethan. "Zombie rats."

Cries of disbelief and excited chatter erupted around the church. Someone in the back yelled, "What do you mean zombie rats?"

"Shut up and he'll explain," shouted Melissa.

Once everyone quieted down again, Nate continued.

"I mean rats that are zombies. An hour ago, Fred and I swung by the Revere Beach community, and the whole place was overrun with them. They had invaded the condo complex and the nursing home. No one survived. At least, I didn't see anyone."

"How do you know they were zombies?" asked Alanna.

"I saw them up close. They were decayed, chunks of flesh

torn from them, their eyes milky white. And they acted like regular zombies do. Once they spotted Fred and me, the pack cried out and attacked."

"How many rats were there?" asked Ethan.

"A fucking ton of them." Nate shrugged. "Thousands. Tens of thousands. Probably hundreds of thousands."

Gasps and chatter erupted from the crowd. Ethan attempted to calm things down.

Alanna stood. "Did they follow you to Nahant?"

Nate shrugged again. "I don't think so. I hauled ass out of there. They were out of view by the time I reached the Lynnway."

Ethan stepped forward. "We have to assume the pack is heading this way and need to figure out a way to stop them."

"You can't kill that many rats," replied Nate.

"No, we can't. We need to figure out a way to repel them."

A middle-aged woman named Shannon stood up, her fear-filled eyes scanning the crowd. "We need to evacuate Nahant before it's overrun like it was five years ago."

Several people agreed with her. Others shook their heads in refusal. Arguments broke out among the crowd.

"No!" Brad shouted, causing the room to go silent. He stood and turned to the crowd. "I evacuated Nahant during the original outbreak. Not this time. We've spent a long time rebuilding this community, and I refuse to abandon it again."

"I don't want to die here," yelled Shannon.

"Then run away. I intend to stand my ground."

Most of the crowd murmured in agreement. Shannon stormed out of the meeting.

Ethan nodded his thanks to Brad. "It's settled. We defend Nahant. But how?"

Deputy Donnelly suggested. "A barricade across the causeway."

A teenager whom Ethan recognized as Connor raised his hand. Ethan pointed to the boy. "Yes?"

Connor stood. "Rats will easily find a way around or over a barricade. It'll barely slow them down."

A young woman behind Connor said, "How the hell do you know that?"

Connor's mother, an extremely attractive blonde with glasses named Kathy, shifted in her chair and glared at the woman. "My son owned rats and has been studying them for years."

The embarrassed woman averted the mother's gaze.

Ethan moved closer to Connor. "Would a trench work?"

"It would slow them down, but considering their numbers, they'd swarm over it."

"Not if we filled it with gasoline and set it on fire," said Brad.

Connor thought for a moment. "That would work."

"How do we build a trench and find gasoline to do this?" asked Sheriff O'Brien. "None of the construction equipment works. Do you expect us to dig this moat by hand?"

"What about the C4?" asked Nate.

Everyone stared at him. Ethan finally asked, "What are you talking about?"

"Don't you remember? A few months ago, I found that stash of C4 while rummaging through the Danvers National Guard armory for supplies. I brought them to you so someone wouldn't steal them and use them inappropriately. Do you still have them?"

Ethan's eyes widened. "I do."

"Can you use them to create the moat?"

"We can," said Brad. "I was trained to use C4 during Operation Freedom Trail. We could get it done in a few hours."

Ethan became excited. "Let's do this."

"Wait a minute." Liz stood. "If we destroy the causeway, how are we going to get to and from the mainland, and how are we going to get supplies to keep the community going?"

"We'll worry about that later," Ethan answered. "If we

don't stop these rats, there'll be no community left."

Liz nodded in reluctant agreement.

Ethan turned to Nate. "Take Brad back to my office to get the C4. Melissa has the keys to the locker."

"Gotcha."

Ethan asked Brad, "How many men will you need to prepare the trench?"

"The more I can get, the quicker we'll be able to prepare the defenses."

Stepping forward, Ethan called out to the group. "I need at least ten volunteers to help build the defenses."

Twenty-one men and women raised their hands.

"Head to the causeway. Brad will meet you there."

"We're going to need tools to break through the asphalt and plant the explosives," suggested Brad.

"There's some at the Nahant Country Club," offered Roger, an older gentleman who oversaw the island's maintenance. "We can use those."

Ethan gave him a thumbs-up. "Have the volunteers gather them and meet us at the causeway."

"Where are we going to get the gasoline?" asked Brad. "After five years, it's all diluted."

"It won't work for driving cars," corrected Nate. "But it's still flammable."

"We can gather the gas." Alanna stood. "The kids and I."

Ethan squinted slightly, displaying uncertainty. "Are you sure?"

Alanna straightened, her smile fading. "We survived the outbreak. I think we're capable of siphoning gas from cars."

Ethan raised his hands in submission. "My bad."

"Check out the marina," said Melissa. "They have a gas pump down there for the boats, though I don't know how full it is. They also have jerry cans in the storeroom, which will make carrying them easy."

"Any questions?" When no one answered, Ethan said. "Alright, let's get moving."

CHAPTER EIGHT

COLONEL WHITAKER WAITED at the end of the parking lot for the Huey to return. General McKinnon stood beside him, doing little to hide his irritation.

"Those assholes better not be fucking around."

"I doubt that, sir." At least, Whitaker hoped that wasn't the case. "The crew is experienced."

"I thought Denning had under a thousand hours of flight time."

"She does, but most of that was after the outbreak. She knows zombies when she sees them."

"I hope so," the general muttered.

When Reynolds reached out to Whitaker half an hour ago to relay the report that zombie rats had broken out of the Boston ZCZ, overrun Winthrop, and were making their way along the coast, he told the radio operator to confirm the message. Reynolds called back a minute later and verified the report. The colonel could not believe it. However, after what had transpired over the last five years, the colonel refused to dismiss it. Since this was a state-wide issue, he called the general so both officers could debrief the crew once they landed.

The thumping of rotor blades sounded from the south, growing louder as the Huey approached the landing zone. Maneuvering over the parking lot, the pilot positioned the helicopter over its designated spot, landed, and shut down the engine. The crew disembarked, removing their flight helmets and talking amongst themselves, a tone of concern in their voices. Whitaker and McKinnon approached the crew, who upon spotting the officers, snapped to attention and saluted.

"At ease," ordered McKinnon. The crew relaxed. "What is this bullshit about ZED rats?"

If Denning was offended, she did not show it. "It's not bullshit, sir. There are hundreds of thousands of them. We saw some on the interior side of the containment wall, but most of the pack was along the coast. They overran the Revere Beach community and were heading north."

"How can you be sure they're ZEDs?" asked Whitaker.

"The stench emanating from the horde was nauseating. Not like what you'd expect from normal rats. More like decayed flesh."

"Plus, the bodies we found scattered around the Winthrop and Revere were stripped clean of flesh," added Libby.

Plati offered the general a camera. "We took photos."

McKinnon scanned through the photos. Whitaker looked over the general's shoulder, muttering, "Jesus Christ."

"That's an understatement." The general handed the camera back to Plati. "Download those photos and forward them to the colonel and me. Then refuel, grab a bite at the cafeteria, and use the bathroom. I want you airborne within an hour to track the horde."

"Yes, sir."

McKinnon turned and headed back to his office.

"What are we going to do about them?" asked Whitaker.

"This is way above my pay grade. We need to contact the President."

CHAPTER NINE

ETHAN GLANCED AT his watch, then back at the crew preparing the road. "This is taking forever."

"We have no other choice," Brad responded. "Without excavation tools, we have to do to it by hand."

Ethan sighed in frustration. He understood that everything needed to be done manually and was grateful that so many residents stepped forward to help. Twenty-one volunteers worked along the track where the trench would be built, using the tools confiscated from the Nahant Country Club. Five of them used pickaxes to break through the asphalt at ten-foot intervals, creating holes two feet in diameter before switching off to dig out the next set. Ten volunteers then used shovels and trowels to dig the holes three feet deep. It had taken almost four hours to prepare enough drill holes to create the trench. The crews were finishing off the last six holes.

Adding to Ethan's frustration, Nate had not arrived yet with the C4.

What wore away at his patience was not so much the preparation time, but his concern that the zombie rats would arrive before the defenses were complete.

Ethan glanced down the causeway toward Nahant. "What the hell is keeping Nate?"

"Relax," answered Brad. "He's only been gone an hour. You don't throw C4 into the back of a pickup like it's an Amazon package. It has to be handled with care."

"I know." Then added, softly, "Sorry."

"Don't apologize. We're all on edge."

A scissor aerial lift sat behind the workforce at the midpoint of the roads leading into Nahant, elevated to its highest level. Melissa and Roberta, one of the police deputies, stood on the platform scanning the roads with binoculars in case the zombie rats approached.

Ethan walked up to the aerial lift. "Any signs of the rats?"

Melissa lowered the binoculars and leaned over the railing. "This is the fifth time you've asked in the past four hours, and the answer is still the same. No." Melissa softened her tone. "Don't worry. We'll let you know if we spot them."

Ethan smiled. Melissa always got snarky with him when he was a pain in the ass. Her mood comforted him.

The volunteers finished creating the last three holes in the asphalt, and a crew moved in to dig them deeper when the sound of a pickup truck engine resonated along the causeway. Ethan turned to see Nate approaching, with Fred's head sticking out the passenger side window, enjoying the ride. Relief washed over him.

He tapped Brad on the shoulder. "Nate's here."

"Perfect timing."

The two men greeted Nate as he pulled his pickup alongside the work area. Nate climbed out, followed by Fred, who ran over to say hello to the volunteers.

"Sorry it took so long to get here," Nate apologized.

"You're just in time." Brad walked over to the bed and peered inside. "How much C4 did you bring?"

"All of it. Thirty-four one-and-a-half-pound blocks."

Brad opened a cardboard box. "Thank God. You also collected detonation cords and detonators. That'll make the job easier."

"Thanks." Nate chuckled. "I'm not as dumb as I look."

"You're far from dumb." Ethan patted his shoulder. "You've been a Godsend getting this community back on its feet."

"And now you saved it from the zombie rats," added Brad.

One of the volunteers taking a break strolled over to the pickup. "Do you guys need help?"

"Thanks." Brad pointed to the C4. "Place one block in front of each hole."

The volunteer climbed into the pickup's bed and waved over five of his buddies, then relayed Brad's order.

"What about the gasoline?" asked Ethan.

"The school kids are gathering it at the pier. Once we unload this stuff, I'll pick up the gas and bring it back."

Brad nodded. "Perfect. The trench should be ready by the time you get back."

It took less than half an hour to unload the pickup. The volunteers placed the remaining four blocks by the aerial lift. Nate called Fred, who was getting belly rubs from Connor. The dog rolled onto his feet and rushed back to the pickup, diving into the open driver's door. Nate climbed behind the wheel, shut the door, and leaned out the window.

"I'm going to the pier now. I should be back within an hour."

Brad nodded. "Perfect."

Ethan and Brad moved away from the pickup as Nate swung it into a tight U-turn and headed back down the causeway.

"What's the next step?" asked Ethan.

"Time to get to work," said Brad.

"Do you need help?"

"I got this. Thanks."

Brad laid the detonator on the ground, picked up the box of detonation cord, and walked over to the hole at the far right of the causeway. All the volunteers joined Ethan, watching Brad as he worked.

Brad shaped the first block of C4 into a flat sheet, completely covering the bottom of the hole with the excess folded up the sides. With the C4 in place, he unraveled a spool of detonation cord, a flexible tube filled with high explosives used as a primer. He then inserted a blasting cap into the C4 and the detonation cord onto the blasting cap. Once primed, he moved on to the next hole, repeating the same process, the cord stretching across the asphalt between them. It took over an hour to place and prime the row of C4. When finished, Brad returned to the others, warning Melissa and Roberta to come down and join them.

"Are we set?" asked Ethan.

Brad nodded. "Have someone grab the extra blocks of C4, then we'll fall back until the spool runs out. I want to put a safe distance between us and the explosions."

Everyone fell back four hundred feet before the spool ran out of cord. Brad attached the cord to the detonator.

"Everyone ready?"

They all replied yes.

"Fire in the hole."

Brad pressed the detonator switch. A series of thirty explosions erupted across the causeway, sending asphalt and dirt skyward and covering the area in smoke. The group spun around and ducked as small debris rained down on them. Once the area had settled down, everyone stood and stared at the end of the causeway, watching as the smoke slowly dissipated. An unsettling silence settled over the crowd.

Brad spoke first. "Let's see if it worked."

Ethan and Brad walked over to the explosion site, with the rest of the group close behind them. When they reached the trench, Ethan whistled.

"God damn. It worked."

"I knew it would."

The explosions had ripped up the causeway, creating a trench nearly five feet deep and ten feet across, creating a barricade from the edge of the inner bay to the shoreline on the opposite side that the rats would have to cross.

"We're all set." Brad turned to face the others. "Once we

douse this with gasoline and light it up, we'll have a firepit that nothing can cross."

JESSICA AND CARISSA exited the shack, each holding two empty jerry cans, Carissa banging hers against the door frame. Jessica gently laid hers down on the pier. Carissa dropped hers in a series of metallic clangs.

Monica glanced at the two girls. "Good job."

"Thanks." Jessica smiled. "There's another half a dozen inside. We'll get them."

"Don't hurry. Kevin hasn't figured out how to get the pump working."

"I'm working on it," Kevin snapped in frustration.

Jessica walked over. "What's the problem?"

"I can't get the gas flowing." Kevin held the nozzle in his left hand while using his right to try to start the pump. After several failed attempts, he slammed the nozzle against the pump, fracturing the pane.

"Let me." Jessica stepped up. Kevin handed her the nozzle and moved back. She examined the pump for a moment, then placed the nozzle back in its slot. "There's your problem. It's electric, not manual."

Kevin rolled his eyes. "That sucks. Now, how are we going to get the gasoline?"

"We'll take it directly from the tank."

"Where's that?"

Jessica pointed to a second shed to the right of the pump. "Probably in there."

She walked over and tried to open the door. "It's locked."

"I got this." Carissa went back to the shack with the jerry cans and exited with an axe. Stepping up to the lock, she smashed it three times until it broke. Carissa removed the shattered lock, opened the door, and gave Kevin a thumbs-up.

"Thanks," he mumbled, embarrassed.

Jessica turned to Carissa. "Bring the jerry cans over here."

Inside stood a five-hundred-gallon tank. Jessica banged her fist on the side. Rather than an echo, she got a dull thud. Moving to the side, she checked the gauge. "There's a hundred gallons left. That should be more than enough."

"We still have no way of getting it out," Kevin complained.

Jessica turned around, pulled a rubber hose from a hook on the wall, and handed it to Kevin. "You need to siphon it out."

"How do you do that?"

Jessica rolled her eyes. She unscrewed the cap on top of the tank, lowered one end of the hose into the tank until it struck the bottom, then handed the other end to Kevin. "Suck on this end until the gasoline starts flowing."

Kevin unscrewed the cap on the jerry can and then began sucking at the end of the hose. A few seconds later, he removed the hose from his mouth, inserted it into the jerry can, and spit out the gasoline in his mouth.

Myles and Heather approached from the pier, Myles rolling a plastic fifty-five-gallon drum while Heather followed behind, clutching her teddy bear.

"Where did you find that?" Jessica asked.

"In the back of the main office," answered Heather. "It's the only thing of use."

"That's fine. Once we fill that and the jerry cans, it should be enough to light the trench on fire. Set it up by the shed."

Heather saluted and followed Myles as he continued rolling the drum down the pier.

"Where's Alanna?" asked Kevin.

"She's checking out the boats."

ALANNA MADE HER way along the pier. Only three boats remained: two rowboats left behind during the evacuation five years ago and a pontoon boat that one of the residents had docked here when they arrived at Nahant in the early days of the community. The rowboats had barely survived, their hulls rusted from years of exposure to the weather, each having several inches of water in them. Even if she dumped out the water, they were in such bad shape she doubted they'd last long enough to escape.

She made her way over to the pontoon boat. In the early days of the settlement, the owners used it to fish and provide food for the residents. Now that they were self-sufficient, it had sat idle for several months. Alanna stepped onto the boat and looked around. Its deck showed some wear and tear, and the leather seats were frayed, but everything else seemed functional, which pleased her. Thankfully, the engine used diesel fuel, so it would still work if any fuel remained. She removed the gas cap from the engine and peeked inside. It was three-quarters full. Perfect.

Even better, the owners had left the key in the ignition. Alanna sat in the driver's seat and studied the console. Once she figured out how to start the engine, she turned the key to the ON position and pressed the START button. It sputtered a few times before dying. She tried again. This time, the engine roared to life. Alanna let it run for half a minute before shutting it down. Thank God it worked. Hopefully, they would not need it.

Alanna agreed to have her kids help out any way they could to defend Nahant, but deep down, she felt their efforts would be in vain. Though she had not told anyone, not even the kids, she had decided that if they could not stop the zombie rats, she refused to let them be killed, especially after what they had gone through in the last five years. If the island defenses failed, she intended to abandon the community and get the kids to a safe location.

Assuming one existed.

Removing the key from the ignition, she slid it under the

driver's seat, then rejoined the others.

Kevin had finished filling the fifty-five-gallon drum and switched the hose to one of the five-gallon cans, jumping to one side as gasoline spilled on the ground.

"Shit. It got on my shoes."

"You'll be fine," joked Alanna. "Just don't play with matches for a while."

"There goes my night," he replied sarcastically.

Alanna stepped up to Kevin and whispered, "Let Myles finish that. I need to talk to you and Jessica."

She strolled over to the parking lot and waited. Kevin gave the hose to Myles, then caught Jessica's attention and nodded his head toward Alanna. The two teenagers joined Alanna.

"What's wrong?" asked Kevin.

"Nothing's wrong. Yet." Alanna pointed to the pontoon boat. "It has a working engine and gasoline. I hid the ignition key under the driver's seat."

Jessica narrowed her eyes. "Why are you telling us this?"

"When the rats reach Nahant, I want you to take the kids to the boat and be ready to evacuate."

"You think the defense trench won't work?" asked Kevin.

"I hope it does. But if it fails, I want you all here ready to evacuate,"

"Why?"

"We spent five years surviving the zombie outbreak. I'm not going to lose any more of you because it broke out again."

Jessica glanced at Kevin, then back at Alanna. "What about the others? We're part of this community."

"If the rats break through the defenses, there'll be no community left. At that point, you're my only concern. In case of a worst-case scenario, you get the hell out of here."

"What about you?" Kevin grew nervous. "Aren't you coming?"

"Yes. But let's be clear on this. If the rats reach the pier before I do, leave without me. Understood?"

Kevin nodded. Jessica mumbled, "Yes."

Nate pulled into the parking lot. Fred stuck his head out the window, barking and wagging his tail when he saw the kids. Nate backed the pickup to the pier, shut off the engine, and climbed out. Fred followed, racing down the pier to the others. Heather called out to him and crouched. Fred ran up, rolled onto his back, and got a belly rub.

Nate approached Alanna and tipped his baseball cap. "I'm here to pick up the gasoline."

"We're almost done. The drum and most of the cans are filled. We'll help you load them."

"I appre—"

Several explosions sounded from northern Nahant, drawing everyone's attention to the noise.

"We'd better hurry," suggested Nate. "They'll need that gas soon."

THE RATS HAD stopped their rampage once the food supply ran out. The pack swarmed just north of the Western Channel that divided Revere and Lynn. Many of the zombie rats had filtered into the nearby stores and restaurants, unsuccessfully rummaging for food that had either spoiled or been looted by survivors.

The rat king sat on the hood of a rusted Honda Civic abandoned on the Lynnway, considering his next move. With the food supply having been exhausted, the horde would soon begin feeding on each other again, which would—

A series of explosions sounded a few miles away, causing its ears to straighten. Noise meant food.

Jumping off the hood of the Honda, the rat king raced across the Lynnway and through the KFC parking lot. The pack fell in behind their leader. After several hundred feet, they reached the shoreline and paused. Across the bay sat a strip of land, smoke rising from the northern end. The king rat stood on its hind legs and sniffed, picking up the odor of food.

The king rat squealed loudly, informing the pack of their next target. Taking the lead, it directed the massive, starving horde north along the shoreline toward Nahant.

CHAPTER TEN

PRESIDENT LISA MARTINETTI sat at her desk, a look of shock and disbelief on her face as she listened to General McKinnon relay the details of the outbreak in Boston over the speakerphone. She had been heading the government-in-exile at White Sands, New Mexico, since the early days of the initial ZED outbreak. There had been no incidents since the taking back of the country concluded almost a year ago. Everything they had spent five years fighting for now threatened to be undone.

General Douglas Meyer, the base commander, sat opposite the President, his expression showing his typical resolve as he scanned through the photos on his laptop that the general had forwarded to him.

"You're absolutely certain these are zombie rats? Most other containment areas have reported a spike in their rodent populations, but none of them have reported the rats having turned."

"I know it sounds insane," replied McKinnon. "The helicopter crew swears by what they saw, and the photos confirm it."

"I agree with the general," said Meyer as he passed the laptop to the President.

Martinetti studied the photos. Her face turned ashen as she realized the dilemma she faced.

After a moment of silence, Meyer asked, "What do you recommend?"

McKinnon paused, then with a trembling voice suggested, "Maybe we should implement Operation Final Thunder."

No one spoke for several seconds as the implication of such an action set in. Meyers spoke first.

"The nuclear option seems a bit extreme."

Martinetti shook her head. "We need to stop this outbreak before it grows out of control."

"I agree with the general," seconded McKinnon. "We have a lot of communities around Boston. The fallout would have devastating consequences. But preventing this outbreak from spreading is our first priority."

"What do you recommend?" Martinetti asked angrily.

"What about Operation Vesta?" suggested Meyer. "The effects on the surrounding communities would be minimal. It would be a major operation, but it should be successful. If not, we could still implement Final Thunder."

Martinetti looked down at the phone. "What do you think, General McKinnon?"

"I concur with the general."

"Then it's settled. I'll order the implementation of Operation Vesta immediately. General McKinnon, I'll give you advanced warning so you can have your guards withdraw to a safe position and prepare your emergency support teams."

"Thank you, Madam President. I'll keep you posted on any changes in the situation."

"I'd appreciate that." Martinetti disconnected the phone call, then focused her attention on Meyer. "What's the next step?"

"I'll contact Pease Air Force Base. They have a squadron of F-18s and Warthogs. It'll be easy to fly everything else we need into the base."

"Thank you." Martinetti sighed and massaged her temples.

Meyer offered support. "You made the right decision."

"I hope so. I don't want to be known as the second president to be responsible for allowing a zombie outbreak in the United States."

CHAPTER ELEVEN

ETHAN STROLLED ALONG the newly-made trench, admiring the results of Brad's explosive expertise. Brad walked to his right, proud of the work he had done, and a little surprised that everything had gone according to plan. If his time in the military taught him anything, it was hope for the best but plan for the worst.

Ethan turned to his friend and nodded. "This trench is great. But will it stop the horde?"

"It will once we fill it with gasoline. That'll create a fire ditch nothing can cross."

"What if the fire dies out before the rats do?"

"I doubt that'll happen."

Truth be told, that was Brad's biggest concern. He had no idea how much gas Alanna and the kids could find. With luck, they would procure enough to cover the length of the trench, or even better, enough to cover the length and add to the fire if it started to go out. The alternative would be that they could not find enough fuel to light the entire trench, with disastrous consequences. Another rule of combat he learned the hard way was that no plan survived first contact with the enemy.

Brad left Ethan to continue his inspection and headed back toward the crowd. With their service no longer needed, several of the volunteers went back to Nahant. Most stayed around, having brought their weapons to help defend the island. Other residents straggled in to watch things as they played out. Brad hoped the zombie rats had already moved on, and they would be wasting their time.

MELISSA AND ROBERTA had resumed their positions atop the elevated lift. Melissa enjoyed it up here. The sun inched toward the horizon, taking with it the unbearable heat and some of the humidity, what remained being dissipated by the cool breeze blowing in from the ocean. She paused to look out over the shoreline. Melissa enjoyed Nahant, having always wanted to reside near the ocean but never being able to afford it. Living here helped ease some of the anxiety of surviving the apocalypse. She prayed that—

"Fuck!" blurted Roberta.

Melissa spun around to see the woman focusing her binoculars along the Lynnway toward Lynn. Her body shook from fear.

"What's wrong?"

"Can't you hear them? They're coming."

Melissa listened. Though distant, she could hear the squeals of rats approaching but had no idea how many and where the noise was coming from.

Melissa leaned over the guardrail and yelled, "They're coming."

FUCK, THOUGHT BRAD. "How far away are they?"

"We hear them approaching from the west but can't see them yet."

"Keep us posted." Ethan sighed frustratedly. "Where the fuck is Nate?"

As if on cue, the pickup's horn beeped several times. They turned to see Nate racing down the causeway, a fifty-five-gallon drum of gasoline and several jerry cans in the bed. Brad breathed a sigh of relief. That should be more than enough to supply the trench.

If it arrived in time.

Nate pulled up to the trench, stopped, and leaned out the window. "I've got the gas—"

"No time for that," called Brad. "They're on their way."

"Shit." Nate jumped out of the cab. Alanna joined him. Fred sat in the cab, barking.

The residents had already removed the jerry cans from the pickup. Brad and Ethan jumped in and maneuvered the large drum to the edge. As the volunteers lowered the drum to the ground, Brad issued orders.

"Start pouring the jerry cans into the trench. Alanna, make a dozen Molotov cocktails."

Everyone sprang into action. Those without jerry cans moved to the edge of the trench, prepared to fight off the horde.

Brad placed the drum on its side, rolled it to the trench, positioned it so the top hung over the edge, and opened the cap. Gasoline poured out. Ethan joined him. Together, the two men rolled it along the trench, soaking the bottom with gasoline.

MELISSA SCANNED THE surrounding roads through her binoculars. Movement to the west caught her attention. She focused her gaze in that direction just as the pack rounded the curve near North Shore Community College and raced down the Lynnway. The sight caused her to gasp. She thought Nate had been exaggerating when describing the pack. If anything, Nate had downplayed its size.

All four lanes of the Lynnway swarmed with zombie rats, the pack stretching back as far as she could see. A tidal wave of decayed flesh and blood-soaked fur bore down on them, the ungodly squealing growing louder by the second. Leading them was a rat the size of a dog. They were half a mile away and approaching fast.

Melissa leaned over the guardrail and yelled, "They're less than half a mile away."

BRAD AND ETHAN continued rolling the drum along the edge, picking up speed. Other volunteers ran past with jerry cans, pouring the contents at the other edge of the trench and moving toward the two men. Brad could smell the rotten stench of the mass. Their squealing drowned out all other sounds. Glancing to his left, he saw them only five hundred feet away.

The two men and the volunteers met up, meaning the entire trench had been soaked. Brad rolled the drum into the breach. Everyone moved away.

Brad screamed, "Light her up!"

Nate picked up a Molotov cocktail, removed a cigarette lighter from his pocket, and lit the rag. The rats had reached the opposite edge of the trench. Many had dived in and climbed up the side. Nate tossed the Molotov cocktail into the trench.

It exploded.

A wall of flame erupted inside the trench, rapidly flowing left and right until the entire length burned furiously. Screeching filled the air as thousands of zombie rats burst into flames. Several dozen breached the top, most on fire. They raced toward the volunteers, making it only a few feet before collapsing, their carcasses in flames. Those that cleared the breach intact were quickly taken down by volunteers with shotguns and semi-automatic weapons.

Despite the flames, the rats continued diving into the trench, oblivious to their imminent death, driven by their obsession with food. The screeching increased in intensity. The stench of burning flesh and organs became overpowering, causing many of the volunteers to vomit.

A screech came from the left. A pack of fifty rats had crossed the far-left portion of the trench before the flames had blocked them and were charging. Nate and Alanna threw Molotov cocktails at them, the explosions igniting most of the rats. Several volunteers rushed toward the survivors, shooting those not on fire. Two unarmed women grabbed shovels and crushed the flaming rodents. Within a minute, the danger had been subdued.

Brad turned his attention back to the trench. Despite the thousands of rats that had already flowed into the flaming depths, the pack pursued its desperate attempt to breach the void. Layers of charred rodent corpses covered the bottom of the trench, rising higher by the minute. The terrifying realization struck him that the rats at the front of the pack were intentionally sacrificing themselves to build a bridge so the others could cross over. At this rate, Nahant would be invaded in minutes.

He ran over to the remaining C4 blocks and searched the cardboard box for shock tubes that would detonate the C4 without primer cord, frustrated that he could not find any.

"Shit!" cried Ethan. "Watch out!"

Brad glanced over his shoulder. Five rats had jumped from the pile over the inner rim, each in flames and surging forward. Two volunteers ran forward, one crushing a rat with his shovel, the other driving a pick into its body. A third volunteer used his shotgun to blast apart the last three.

Rummaging through the box, Brad found a smaller one beneath spools of det cord. Opening it, he breathed a sigh of relief. Inside was a spool of time fuse, which would work just as well. Grabbing the small box and the C4 blocks, he raced back to the trench.

More rats were crossing, all of them being stopped by the frantic efforts of the volunteers. If he didn't act soon, more would cross than could be halted.

Brad used his pocketknife to cut four segments from the

time fuse, which he estimated would burn for approximately five seconds. At least he hoped so. If the fuse went off sooner, it could blow him up. Once he had the time fuses set on the C4, he called out, "Nate, I need your lighter?"

Nate ran over, pulled the lighter from his pocket, and handed it to Brad.

"Thanks." Nate flicked it on and lit the time fuse. "Everyone, fall back."

As the volunteers withdrew, Brad tossed the C4 into the trench. Three seconds later, an explosion rocked the area. Hundreds of zombie rats erupted skyward, falling back to earth in a rain of flaming decay. Most were dead. Those still alive, stunned or crippled, were quickly disposed of by the volunteers. Most importantly, the top layers of burnt rats inside the trench had been cleared, preventing the others from jumping the gap.

The pack kept charging.

Brad grabbed the second block of C4 and checked the trench. The layer had begun rising again. Several rats were again crossing the edge, being taken down by the volunteers. Lighting the fuse on one of the blocks, Brad tossed it into the trench. A few seconds later, it exploded, sending another cloud of flaming rodents raining down on the causeway and clearing away the layer of charred rats.

The rats continued their assault.

Ethan picked up one of the jerry cans still filled with gasoline, brought it up to the edge of the trench, removed the cap, and began pouring its contents into the fire. The flames erupted, the heat forcing Ethan to back away, but not before tossing the jerry can into the fire. It exploded, spreading flames on the opposite edge of the trench.

Several volunteers joined Ethan, each grabbing a filled jerry can and pouring its contents across the trench. The flames shot skyward, accompanied by the intensifying screams of burning rodents and a spike in the stench of charred, decayed flesh.

The pack still surged forward.

Ethan stepped over to Brad. "What are we going to do? They're still coming."

"Have everyone who's not carrying a weapon fall back to Nahant. And tell Nate to start the truck in case the rest of us have to escape in a hurry."

As Ethan issued the directives, Brad moved closer to the trench. Charred skin, seared bones, and dried flesh covered the bottom. Rats continued rushing in, becoming engulfed in flames and shriveling to death. The increased intensity of the flames from the added gasoline slowed them, but only temporarily. He watched the rats that dived into the trench fail to jump the height to the surface, tumbling back down to be consumed in the conflagration, slowly increasing the height of the dead detritus. After several minutes, the rats trying to breach the barrier were getting dangerously close to the lip. Brad stepped back several yards, lit the fuse on the third block, and tossed the C4 at the outer wall. When it exploded, a hundred-foot section of the trench's opposite side collapsed, sending even more rodents to their deaths and widening the gap between the rats and their food.

Ethan stepped up beside Brad. "It looks like that worked."

"But for how long?"

A loud squeal from the opposite side of the trench interrupted Brad. The horde stopped their attack and turned to face the rat king, which jumped off the car roof and raced back down the Lynnway toward Lynn. The pack fell in behind him, abandoning their attack on the causeway.

Ethan called out to Melissa on top of the elevated lift. "What's going on?"

"They're falling back."

"All of them?"

"All that's left."

"How many did we eliminate?" asked Brad.

"Hang on." Melissa raised her binoculars and watched the

rodents as they retreated. "It's hard to tell, but I would say we killed half of them."

Ethan turned to Brad, "That's good, right?"

"So long as they don't try again. We've used up all but one block of C4, a few Molotov cocktails, a shitload of ammo, and all the gasoline. If there's a second assault, we're screwed."

Nate came up, having overheard the conversation. "If you want, I can take Alanna and the kids around the island and gather more gasoline in case they attack again."

"Where would you get it from?" asked Brad.

"There's plenty of abandoned cars around. We'll check each one and hopefully get lucky."

Ethan nodded his approval. "Sounds good to me."

"I agree." Stepping back a few paces, Brad lifted his head. "Melissa, can you still see the rats?"

"No. It looks like they retreated all the way back to downtown Lynn."

"Let's hope they stay there," muttered Ethan.

"But we have to be prepared in case they don't. Nate, gather as much gas as you can and bring it back here. Ethan, I recommend establishing a twenty-four-hour guard. Two people on the elevated lift and two along the trench so they can set it on fire again if necessary. I'd also supply them with any ammo we have left to fend off an attack until help arrives. Agreed?"

Both men replied in the affirmative.

As Ethan and Nate headed off to perform their tasks, Brad strode back to the trench. The flames had died down. The pit was covered in ashes and charred carcasses, lit by the glow of red embers burning beneath. It reminded him of images of Hell which, under the circumstances, were not far from the truth.

They had been fortunate to drive the horde back the first time. He knew a second attack would more than likely succeed. With luck, the rats would move on.

CHAPTER TWELVE

"WHAT ARE WE doing here?" asked Libby. "We're recon, not combat."

Denning rolled her eyes. "I told you twice already. We're here to brief the pilots on what we observed."

"Stop your bitching," added Plati. "This is impressive to watch."

Denning could not argue. She had not seen an operation this large since the containment began.

Nine Navy FA-18 Hornets and eleven Air Force A-10 Thunderbolt IIs, more commonly referred to as Warthogs, sat in line along the tarmac being serviced by ground crews. A C-5 Galaxy transport had parked near the fighters, its ramp lowered. Pallets of aerial weapons were being wheeled off the transport. Denning thought they looked more like missiles than bombs, each weapon ten feet long and smooth along the surface except for four adjustable tailfins. Ground crews attached three bombs to the underbelly and wings of the Hornets and two to the wings of the Warthogs.

"What types of bombs are those?" asked Libby.

Denning shrugged. "I've never seen them before."

"Who cares," said Plati. "The guns on those Warthogs will wreak havoc on those rats."

Denning nodded in agreement. The primary weapons on the Warthogs were GAU-8 Avenger Gatling-style cannons that could fire three thousand nine hundred 30mm rounds a minute. She had seen these weapons used during the Battle of

Albany. They devastated the ZEDs.

A second C-5 sat at the far end of the runway, parked in front of ten C-130 Hercules transport aircraft. Flight crews unloaded a bomb from the C-5 that was thirty feet long and over three feet in diameter. It had twin stabilizers on its flanks and four square-shaped fins at its base.

"Holy shit," mumbled Plati. "Is that what I think it is?"

"Yup." Denning nodded. "It's a MOAB."

Libby glanced between the two officers. "What's a MO-AB?"

"The Mother of All Bombs." Plati patted Libby's shoulder. "That bastard, my friend, holds over eighteen thousand pounds of explosives. It's a massive anti-personnel weapon. Those rats are going to wish they stayed in Boston."

An attractive female Air Force officer in fatigues walked up to them. "Captain Denning?"

"Yes."

"General Ferguson is ready to see you."

She led the three to a small building on the opposite end of the runway of Pease Air Force Base II. Pease had been a major airfield during the Cold War. After the fall of the Soviet Union, the base had been privatized. During Operation Freedom Trail, it had been reclaimed by the military for anti-ZED operations in the region.

Once in the building, the woman led them down a long corridor, stopping in front of a metal door. She opened it and ushered them inside.

Denning realized they had been led to a ready room. She was surprised to see thirty Air Force and Navy pilots seated in the front rows. A tall man with a dark-haired crew cut and a chiseled face stood before the pilots, his demeanor stern. He wore the stars of a brigadier general. On hearing Denning's crew enter, he turned to greet them.

The three snapped to attention and saluted.

Brigadier General Ferguson smiled. "No need for formalities." He stepped over and shook their hands. "Thank you for taking the time to brief us."

"Our pleasure, sir." Denning did not know how to respond since they had been ordered to attend.

Ferguson turned to the pilots. "These are the men and women who will launch the offensive against the ZED rats. Please brief them on what you witnessed."

Denning and her crew spent the next hour briefing the room on the ZED rats, explaining the extent of the carnage caused and where they were located, and answering more than a dozen questions. When finished, Ferguson stood and faced his pilots.

"Okay, ladies and gentlemen, you now know what you're facing. We strike tomorrow at 0700." The general turned to Denning. "You'll be over the target area at 0630 to assess the situation and update us on any changes in the ZED's location."

"Yes, sir."

"Good luck."

Everyone filed out, several of the pilots thanking Denning's crew for providing useful intelligence. Once back at their Huey, Denning paused and studied the line of aircraft.

Plati patted him on the shoulder. "Everything okay, boss?"

"Yeah, I'm just thinking about the hell these guys are going to unleash tomorrow."

CHAPTER THIRTEEN

THE RATS HAD fallen back to Lynn Heritage State Park at the far end of the Lynnway, regrouping after losing half their numbers. Most milled around. A few unsuccessfully searched for food, everything edible having long since been devoured or rotted. The king rat moved amongst its subjects as if it felt defeated over losing so many during the failed attempt to storm Nahant. Or perhaps it merely regretted losing so many of its numbers, significantly decreasing the pack's strength.

The sun set, casting the park into darkness.

Something unusual attracted the king rat's attention. Breaking away from the others, it crossed the park to the pier extending out into the bay, moving along the wooden structure and stopping at the end.

Less than a mile away, lights switched on across Nahant, reminding the king rat that the food was still there.

It stood on its hind legs and squealed. The pack raced down the pier and gathered around the leader. The king rat dove into the water and swam toward Nahant, followed by tens of thousands of zombie rats.

CHAPTER FOURTEEN

ROBERTA AND USMAN, a former Marine who fought the ZED war from day one of the outbreak, stood on top of the elevated lift erected behind the trench, scanning the horizon for the return of the zombie pack. Not that they would spot the attackers until they were practically upon them. Since this part of the island was uninhabited, no efforts had been made to repair the broken streetlamps. Thankfully, a gibbous moon slowly ascended above the ocean, providing enough light to spot the vermin if they tried another raid. All they needed was a few minutes. Roger and Dylan, one of the newest residents who used to teach in Manchester before the apocalypse, stood guard over the trench. The few remaining jerry cans of gasoline were lined up along the edge, ready to be poured in at a moment's notice, with half a dozen Molotov cocktails lined up alongside them. The trench could be activated in less than a minute.

"Hey, Bertha," Dylan called out.

"It's Roberta."

"Sorry." Embarrassment seeped into his voice. "I'm still learning everyone's names."

"Apology accepted. What do you need?"

"Can you toss down two bottles of water for Roger and me?"

"I got this," said Usman. Turning around, he reached into the cooler and removed two bottles, then leaned over the guardrail. "Ready?"

"Yes."

Usman dropped the bottles one at a time. After releasing the second one, Dylan shouted, "Damn."

"You okay?"

"Yeah. I missed it, and it hit my face."

At that moment, the two-way radio on Roberta's hip came to life, and Ethan's voice came over the speaker.

"Roberta, are you there?"

She removed it and pressed the TALK button. "I'm here."

"Just checking to see if everything is okay."

"It's quiet as a graveyard." Roberta paused. "Probably a poor choice of words."

Ethan laughed. "Hopefully, it will be for the rats. Let me know if you need anything."

"I will." Roberta slipped the radio back on her belt and checked her watch. Only an hour left until her shift was over.

SADIE PLACED THE ceramic mermaid in the center of the bedroom bureau, adjusted it for several seconds, then stepped back to admire it.

Brad slipped up behind Sadie, wrapped his arms around her waist, and kissed her on the cheek. "That really makes you happy."

She cupped his hands with her own. "You have no idea."

"I didn't know you liked mermaids."

"I don't."

"Then why did you want it so much?"

Sadie sighed and held his hand tighter. "My mother was a mermaid collector. She had an entire cabinet in her living room. This one looks a lot like her favorite."

Brad hugged her. "Sorry that I gave you crap about getting it."

"It's not your fault. I never told you about my experiences

during the outbreak."

"I'm ready to listen if you ever want to."

"Not yet.

Sadie turned around, took Brad's head in her hands, and passionately kissed him for several seconds. When Sadie broke the kiss, she took Brad's hand and led him to the bed.

"Are you going to thank me for getting it for you?"

"Nope." Sadie glanced at him with lust in her eyes. "I need some rough sex to keep me grounded."

NATE LOADED THE thirteenth jerry can of gasoline into the bed of his pickup. Fred stood in the back, sniffing each of the cans, barking his approval.

Alanna came over with another can and loaded it in the bed, then scratched Fred behind the ears.

"How are we doing?" asked Nate.

"The kids have collected five more cans and are filling the last three."

"Good."

Kevin, Jessica, and Carissa walked up with five cans, the siblings each carrying two and Carissa struggling with the fifth. Heather followed, hugging her teddy bear. They placed the cans by the pickup, each one pausing to catch their breath.

Nate nodded. "You guys are doing a great job."

Kevin smiled. "Thanks. But we're exhausted. How much longer do we have to do this?"

"We'll stop once these cans are filled," Nate replied. "This should be enough to stop another attack."

Heather clasped the teddy bear against her chest. "Hopefully we won't need it."

"Amen," Jessica said under her breath.

As Nate and Alanna loaded the cans in the pickup, Myles walked up with two more.

"How are you keeping track of the cars you've already hit?" asked Nate.

Myles shrugged.

Kevin answered. "We're leaving the lids open and not reattaching the caps."

"Makes sense." After loading the cans in the back, Nate asked, "Who are we missing?"

Alanna pointed farther down the street. "Just Monica. She's filling the last can."

"Once she's done, I'll drop you off at your house, then I'll take these to the trench."

LIZ SAT IN Alanna's chair, with Myeong-hwa, Debbie, and Sean seated in school chairs in a circle in front of her. The kids were traumatized after the events of that afternoon, so Liz thought she'd comfort them by cooking sloppy joes in the school cafeteria and then reading to them for a few hours. Since the oldest was only ten, she chose a selection of Dr. Seuss books she had found in the ransacked school library. She had already read *The Cat in the Hat* and *Go, Dogs, Go* and had started reading *Green Eggs and Ham.*

Halfway through the third page, Myeong-hwa raised her hand. "Excuse me, Miss Liz."

"Yes?"

"Where do you get green eggs? I've never seen one before."

Sean rolled his eyes. "There's no such thing as green eggs."

Myeong-hwa seemed confused. "Then why did he write about them?"

"It's a children's book," replied Sean. "It's not real."

"It's like the last book," added Debbie. "Have you ever seen a talking dog driving a car?"

"Fred."

Sean rolled his eyes again. "Fred doesn't talk."

"Yes, he does," Myeong-hwa responded. "He just speaks in dog language. And he drives Nate's truck."

"He rides in Nate's truck."

Liz interrupted the debate. "Myeong-hwa, it's always good to ask questions. That's how you learn things. And yes, Sean is right, it's only a children's book, so the author fictionalizes things to make it interesting." She shot a disapproving glance at Sean. "Even if we disagree with someone, we need to be more respectful of their opinions."

Sean lowered his head. "Sorry, Miss Liz."

"You don't need to apologize to me."

Sean looked over at Myeong-hwa. "Sorry."

She smiled. "It's okay."

Liz resumed reading.

ETHAN STARED AT the two-way radio on top of his desk, waiting for it to come to life with a report that the zombie rats were back, while praying that it wouldn't. Though he would not admit it publicly, he felt their success this afternoon was a fluke. They had used up all of their C4, most of the gasoline, and way too much ammunition, yet destroyed only half of the pack. If the rats attempted to invade again, he doubted they had enough resources to push them back a second time.

Ethan had lost everything during the outbreak five years ago, including his family, whom he loved more than anything else. Not knowing if they had died or were lost in a relocation to a safer area, and if they had passed, not knowing whether or not they suffered, tore him apart emotionally. He would never get over the heartbreak. The thought of losing everything all over again nauseated him. A part of him wanted to ask God to protect the community and keep them safe, but he had forgone his faith during the first weeks of the apocalypse, and the crisis they faced now only reassured his belief that a divine being did not exist.

A knock on the door startled Ethan. He sat upright, nearly falling out of his chair. It took a second for his nerves to calm, then he said, "Come in."

Melissa opened the door and stuck her head inside. Her grin faded when she saw the look on Ethan's face.

"Sorry. Did I startle you?"

"Yes, but it's not your fault. My mind is focused on those rats."

"Obsessed is more like it." Her tone sounded more supportive than accusatory.

"I'm worried that something… no, terrified that something might happen to the compound. We've worked too hard to build Nahant to have it collapse again."

Melissa stepped inside and moved over to the desk. "You've gone above and beyond to make Nahant a safe place to live. The appearance of these rats is not your fault. I doubt we would have survived this afternoon's attack without your leadership."

"You're saying that because I'm your boss," Ethan joked.

"I'm saying that because it's true. I hear the gossip around town. These people respect you and appreciate all you've done for them. Barterville is a huge success. Everyone in the surrounding communities wants to move here."

It felt good to hear. Ethan needed the support right now. "Thank you."

"Do you need me to get you anything?" Melissa asked.

"I'm fine, thanks. It's getting late, though. Why don't you go home?"

"Are you sure?"

"Yes. You had a long day."

Melissa chuckled. "We all did."

She made her way to the door. Before leaving, she turned to Ethan. "You know that radio will work just as well from your house as it will from here."

"I know. But if I take this to my place, I'll feel like I'm bringing my work home with me."

Melissa smiled. "Take care of yourself. We need you."

"You, too. I'll see you in the morning."

"WE'RE ALMOST THERE," urged Deputy Donnelly. He held Gina's hand, keeping her balance as they made their way through the woods up the hill.

"Slow down. You're going too fast."

"My bad." He lovingly squeezed her hand, reassured when she returned the gesture.

"This better be worth it."

"Oh, it will be."

Gina flashed him a look that was half frustrated, half humorous. "I mean the view."

Donnelly laughed. "That, too."

After another two minutes of climbing, the couple finally reached the top. Gina bent over and huffed, breathing deep. "I haven't had a workout like that in a while."

Hopefully, we'll both get an even better one before the night is over, the deputy thought. He placed his hands on Gina's shoulders and slowly spun her around, keeping them there.

"Was it worth it?"

Gina gasped excitedly. "Definitely. The view is beautiful."

From the top of the hill where Fort Ruckman was located, they could see all of Nahant stretched out before them. The few working streetlamps and the glow coming from residences made the island appear serene, enhanced by the lights coming from the houses near the shore reflecting off the water. A sliver of white light from the rising moon stretched across the ocean, adding to the romance of the setting.

"I never realized how lovely Nahant is until now," said Gina. "It's beautiful."

"Like you."

Gina looked over her shoulder and smiled flirtatiously. "Deputy Donnelly, did you bring me up here to seduce me?"

"Never," he replied sarcastically.

"Bummer." She kissed his hand on her shoulder and turned her attention back to Nahant. "And if you listen, you can hear the waves crashing along the shoreline."

Donnelly leaned forward and listened. With the noise from cars no longer an issue, the sound of the breaking waves overrode all other sounds. It was romantic, setting the mood for a night of—

Another sound from the western side of the island interrupted the serenity. Donnelly and Gina focused their attention on the noise, watching as a black mass rushed out of the water.

"Oh my God!" exclaimed Gina.

Donnelly pulled the two-way radio off his belt and pressed the TALK button.

"Sheriff, we have an emergency. The rats are invading along the west coast."

O'BRIEN CRUISED ALONG Castle Road, the coastal road running along the western edge of Nahant. He drove an old diesel-powered 1969 Land Rover that Nate had discovered a month ago among several vintage cars in a garage in Rockport. Nate made some minor repairs to it and donated the Land Rover to the sheriff's department. It was old. O'Brien had to teach himself how to use a stick shift and needed to lower the windows manually, but at least it allowed him to do patrols and respond quickly—

An unusual sound broke through the silence of the night, sending a cold chill down the sheriff's spine. He shifted into PARK and turned off the engine. Flashbacks to earlier that day raced through his mind as squeals of zombie rats cut through the night. The motherfuckers must have swam across the bay.

A large mass of zombie rats swarmed across the street ten feet in front of him. Most of the pack raced across the road into Nahant, led by the giant rat king. Several hundred noticed the sheriff and lunged toward him.

O'Brien rolled up the driver's window, then leaned across the front seat to do the same on the passenger side. The rats swarmed over the Land Rover. One pushed its way through the passenger window, the sheriff catching it between the glass and the upper frame. Removing his .38 caliber revolver from its holster, O'Brien shot it in the face, blowing its head off. The shattered corpse fell backward into the street. He finished closing it.

By now, the rats had covered the windshield, blocking his view. O'Brien started the engine, shifted into DRIVE, and slammed his foot on the accelerator. The crunching of rodents and their death squeals filled the vehicle. He spun the steering wheel to the left and back again, the sudden swerve throwing off most of the rats.

"Shit!" A stalled Audi Q5 sat ten feet in front of him.

O'Brien whipped the steering wheel to the right. He raced past the Audi, its front bumper tearing a gash in the driver's door but not stopping the Land Rover. More rats fell off the roof and windshield. The sheriff increased his speed, continuing to crush the rodents under his tires as he sped away.

Donnelly's voice came over the radio. "Sheriff, we have an emergency. The rats are invading along the west coast."

O'Brien picked up the radio and pressed the TALK button. "No fucking shit. I'm caught in the middle of it."

A loud pop came from the front right as the tire blew, sending the Land Rover swerving to one side. O'Brien corrected the steering wheel and increased speed, needing to escape the pack before they overwhelmed him.

"What should we do?" asked Donnelly over the radio.

O'Brien ignored him, concentrating on getting himself to safety.

The left rear tire blew, the noise of metal rims scraping against asphalt competing with the rats' squeals. Then the right rear tire blew. The fucking rats were taking out his tires.

"Boss, are you okay?"

O'Brien gunned the engine, broke through the edge of the pack, and continued down Castle Road, the Land Rover bucking back and forth as if he was riding a horse in a rodeo.

"Boss, answer me."

O'Brien grabbed the radio and pressed the TALK button. "I'm fine. The pack nearly took me out, but I broke free."

"Were you bitten?"

"Thank God, no."

"What are we going to do?"

O'Brien paused a second before responding. "There's no way to stop them. We have to get as many people to safety as possible."

Glancing in the rearview mirror, he saw hundreds of crushed rats, but nowhere near enough to save Nahant. A few dozen chased the Land Rover, quickly falling behind. One large swarm broke off and headed toward the causeway. The majority of the pack still swarmed across the road into Nahant.

MELISSA TOOK A slow walk home, enjoying the cool breeze wafting in from the ocean and the briny smell it brought. Every now and then, a wave crashed hard enough on the shoreline that she could hear the rumble from here.

She hated leaving Ethan alone, but by now had gotten used to his stubbornness. Okay, that was not the correct way to describe it. For as long as she had known him, he had dedicated his life to building a society in Nahant that would give its residents hope for the future. It derived from his business acumen from the days before the outbreak. He often worked twelve to sixteen hours a day to sustain the community.

Everyone owed their life to him, especially after today's near catastrophe. She planned to get a good sleep and go in early tomorrow. If Ethan was still there, she would adopt her motherly attitude and send him—

Another sound cut through the night, only this time not the relaxing crashing of waves against the shore. This one terrified Melissa. She heard the scampering of thousands of tiny feet followed by increasing, ungodly squeals. A moment later, she smelled the stench of rotten flesh.

Being closer to her house than the city hall, Melissa broke into a frantic run, hoping to get home before the pack reached her. She had covered a hundred feet when the squealing became frenzied. Looking over her shoulder, she saw the pack swarm across Bay View Avenue and disperse across Nahant. The four-foot-long, grotesque king rat noticed her and gave chase, followed by several dozen of its followers.

Melissa screamed and ran for her life.

She heard a loud squeal then, a moment later, the king rat landed on her back, its size and weight knocking her to the ground. She fell face-first onto the asphalt, breaking her jaw and fracturing three of her front teeth. The smell of blood drove the zombie rats crazy.

Rolling over, Melissa knocked the king rat off her back. Before she could get up, the rest of the mini pack dove on top of her and began to feed, ripping through her clothes and tearing chunks out of her skin. She screamed as much from terror as agony. One rat ate its way through the skin of her abdomen, sank its teeth into her intestines, and ripped them out of her body. Seven rats began feeding on the dislodged organ.

The king rat jumped on Melissa's chest and lowered its face close to hers. She saw the half-eaten face and milky eyes inches away. With a gut-wrenching squeal, it wrapped its mouth around her lower jaw and pulled back, tearing the bone from its sockets and tearing out her tongue. Melissa tried to scream, but the blood flowing down her esophagus prevented her from doing so. The king rat tossed the severed jaw to one side, then plunged its jaw deep into Melissa's mouth, chewing on the back of her throat.

SHANNON STRETCHED OUT on her sofa, doing what she enjoyed best: reading. It was her relief after the disastrous town meeting earlier that day. She had the windows open, enjoying the cool breeze blowing from the ocean. Being forty-eight and slightly deaf, Shannon could not hear the approaching squeals of the zombie rats.

However, Melissa's agonizing screams broke through the silence, startling Shannon. She placed a bookmark between the pages she was reading, put the novel on the sofa, and crossed the living room. Opening the front door, she stepped out onto the porch.

"Do you need help?"

Melissa did not answer.

Moving onto the front porch and descending the steps to the front lawn, Shannon called out, "Is anyone out there?"

A second later, she heard the squealing of the zombie rats. Attracted by the noise, a group broke away from the path and rushed toward Shannon.

"Shit!"

Shannon spun around and raced back to her house. She tripped over the second step and crashed onto the porch, shattering her ankle. Her scream of pain was cut off when the rats covered her, scores of them stripping away her flesh and burrowing into her organs.

FROM THE TOP of the elevated lift, Roberta heard rats squealing in the distance. Fear wracked her body. Raising the binoculars, she scanned the Lynnway and the beach road but saw nothing.

"Did you hear that?" Roger yelled up to her.

"Yes. But I can't see them."

Usman tapped her shoulder and pointed down the causeway. "That's because they're already in Nahant."

Roberta moved to the other side of the lift and raised the binoculars. Several thousand rats ran down the causeway heading toward them. They had at most a minute to defend themselves.

"What are we going to do?" asked Dylan.

Roger ran over to the jerry cans and grabbed two. "We'll make a ring of fire around us. That should hold them back."

Roberta removed the two-way radio and pressed the TALK button. "This is Roberta at the trench site. We have zombie rats approaching our position from the causeway. I repeat, we have rats approaching our position from the causeway. Somehow, they circumvented our defenses."

Usman switched his attention between the zombie rats and Roger. Roger retrieved the cans and brought them to Dylan, who emptied them, creating a circle that stretched from the trench, around the lift, and back to the trench. When they completed the circle, Usman looked back at the rats.

They were one hundred feet away and closing rapidly.

"Hurry up. They're here."

Roger and Dylan each grabbed a Molotov cocktail, lit the rags, and tossed them onto opposite sides of the circle. Flames ignited, creating a wall of fire just as the rats reached the team.

Dylan hand-pumped the air. "Fuck you, assholes."

Rather than rush into the flames as before, the pack veered to their left.

"The bastards are retreating." Roger turned and fist bumped Dylan.

Usman knew that was not the case but was unable to stop it.

The rats dove into the trench, ran down to the section between the circle, and began piling on top of each other. A moment later, a dozen rats breached the trench's rim and rushed toward Roger and Dylan.

Roger picked up the last Molotov cocktail, lit it, and threw it into the swarm. Squeals of agony erupted as the rats ignited, burning off their decayed flesh and cooking their rotted organs. The few rats on fire that made it through were easily killed by the two men.

More rats breached the top of the pit and swarmed around the burning pile of their comrades.

Roger froze in fear, instantly being overrun. He fell to his knees as the vermin tore into him. Two rats chewed out his eyes, then dug into the sockets, one of them doing so with such force that it fractured his skull. The rest covered his back, chest, arms, and legs, ravaging their prey. Roger's screams morphed into psychotic laughter as he went insane from the pain. A few seconds later, Roger fell face-first onto the ground, dead. The rats stripped his body clean of flesh and organs.

Dylan backed away until he felt the flames singeing his back. He knew it was a futile attempt. A rat lunged at his face. Dylan slapped it away. A dozen more rats attacked, landing on his chest and legs and knocking him into the flames. The clothes seared off his body in seconds. The skin, muscles, and tissues burned more slowly as the intense heat evaporated the water within him. Once Dylan's body and those of the rats dried out, the epidermis caught fire, burning off and peeling away. The blood in their veins and arteries dried out and clotted, clogging their circulatory system. A few seconds later, those same veins and arteries began to melt. Next, the dermis caught fire, shrinking under the heat and bursting open, the fissures leaking fat from Dylan and the rats onto the road. Dylan died, the flames extinguishing the agony of being eaten alive. The rats, on the other hand, despite burning to death, consumed as much of Dylan as was still edible. Eventually, the charring of every part of their bodies took their lives. The rats stopped flaying about.

A few rats found the wooden ladder leading up to the lift and began climbing. Usman noticed them as they neared the top.

"Push the ladder away."

Roberta looked confused. "But then we'll be stuck up here,"

"Better to be stranded up here than eaten alive."

Roberta moved over and shoved the ladder. It fell backward and crashed onto the asphalt, dislodging three rats that fell into the flames.

When the rats had finished stripping Roger and Dylan clean, they ran back to the trench, dove in, and swarmed out the other end, making their way back to Nahant.

Usman hunched over and sighed. "Thank God. We're safe for now."

Roberta stared toward Nahant. "What about the rest of the island?"

"WHAT'S ALL THAT noise?" asked Myeong-hwa.

"You stay here while I check it out," said Liz.

Liz left the classroom, rushed down the corridor, and pushed open the school's front door. She gasped and placed her hands over her mouth to stifle a scream.

Thousands of zombie rats filled the area in front of the school. They flowed in from the bay, racing between the residences along the shore and spanning out across Castle Road. Off to the left, rats swarmed Sheriff O'Brien's Land Rover as he tried to escape the pack, crushing scores of them beneath his tires. Despite all their efforts, the outbreak had reached Nahant. None of the residents would make it out alive.

A squeal came from the pack as several of the rats smelled

Liz's presence and charged.

Liz slammed the door, locked it, and ran back to the classroom. With the rats circling around the school, she had no way to get the kids to safety. However, there was a slim chance she could keep them alive until the crisis concluded.

Bursting into the classroom, she saw the kids standing by the windows and watching the pack surround the building, Debbie shaking in fear. The kid screamed at the noise of the door banging open.

Myeong-hwa spun around. "Miss Liz, where did the rats come from?"

Liz ignored the question. "Follow me."

"Where are we going?" asked Sean.

"Downstairs."

"But they'll find us there."

Liz tapped down her anger but kept her voice firm. "Move!"

The three kids ran out into the corridor and followed Liz. The sound of shattering glass echoed through the building, followed by the rats' squeals as they poured inside.

Reaching the basement door, Liz shoved it open and ushered the kids through. As the last one ran past, rats rushed around the corner and rushed toward them. Closing the door, Liz turned to the kids.

"Hurry up."

"I c-can hear them," Debbie stumbled over her words.

"We'll be fine if we keep moving."

At the bottom of the stairs was a steel door with a worn, rusted sign showing a black circle on a yellow background, with three yellow triangles painted inside the circle, and the words FALLOUT SHELTER beneath it. Liz yanked it open and ushered the kids inside. She heard the sound of the rats crashing through the wooden door upstairs and flowing down the stairs. Liz jumped into the shelter, shut the door, and spun the ship-style wheel that drove the locking bolts into the steel frame. A moment later, rats crashed into the door, the sound reverberating through the shelter.

Debbie broke down and cried. "They'll eat their way through and get us."

"No, they won't." Liz knelt and hugged Debbie. "This is a fallout shelter. It's made of steel and concrete. They can't eat through that."

"What's a fallout shelter?" Myeong-hwa asked.

"They were built during the Cold War to protect students in the event of a nuclear war?"

Sean looked confused. "What's the Cold War?"

"What's a nuclear war?" added Myeong-hwa.

Liz smiled. "I'll teach you about that once this is over. Now let's have a group hug."

All four huddled together and hugged. Liz tried to block out the rats scratching at the steel door.

O'BRIEN CRUISED THROUGH the streets, blaring the Land Rover's horn and warning the residents to run, yelling over the infuriating noise of the vehicle's tire rims chewing against the asphalt.

No one heard him. O'Brien wished he had a real police car with sirens and a loudspeaker.

A middle-aged woman ran out of her house into the street, waving down O'Brien. He recognized her as Cynthia, the community's nurse. She ran up to the open window and leaned in, her eyes wide with concern.

"Sheriff, all I can hear is people screaming. What's going on?"

"The zombie rats invaded the island."

"I thought you stopped them."

"We did. They swam across the bay and came in on the west coast."

The concern in her eyes morphed into terror. "How are we going to kill them?"

"We can't. They've already overrun half the island. Haul ass out of here and get to safety."

"Where is it safe?"

O'Brien did not have an answer. "Your best bet is to head for the coast and swim north to Swampscott. I'm sorry." He hated leaving her alone, but he needed to warn the rest of the residents. "I have to get going."

O'Brien pulled away, trying to ignore Cynthia as she called after him to help her.

Turning tight off Gardner Road onto Trimountain Road, O'Brien slammed on the brakes when Donnelley ran in front of the car. The sheriff stepped out of the vehicle.

"Where the hell were you?"

The deputy ignored the question, giving the sheriff a look that plainly said *What the fuck does it matter now?* "How are we going to stop them?"

"We can't. We need to warn people in enough time to get to safety. Get in."

A man and a woman holding an infant ran up to them. O'Brien recognized them as Vinnie and Martha Lee. O'Brien agreed to be the child's godfather at the christening a few weeks ago. Martha Lee attempted to calm her screaming child. Vinnie shook from fear.

"Sheriff, where's a safe place to hide?"

He sighed. "There are none on the island."

Martha Lee paused, comforting her baby. "What do you mean? You haven't set up a shelter?"

"We never thought we'd need one," snapped O'Brien.

Vinnie and Martha Lee stared at him, shocked. Finally, she said, "What should we do?"

Before O'Brien could respond, Donnelly responded, "Head to the beach."

Both parents turned to him. "What?"

Donnelly pointed east. "Head to Stony Beach."

"Is there a boat there?" asked Vinnie.

"There's nothing there."

"Then why send us?" yelled Martha Lee.

"Because it's your only chance of getting off Nahant. Get to the beach and then swim north to Swampscott. Hopefully, you'll be safe there."

"But…." Martha Lee glanced at Vinnie, then back at Donnelly. "That's too far to swim."

"Then stay here and die." O'Brien slid into the front seat.

Donnelly stepped up to the couple and spoke softly. "It's your only chance. Head there before the rats take over the entire island. And good luck."

He ran to the passenger side and climbed in. O'Brien continued down the street, both men yelling for the residents to run while they had a chance.

"WHAT THE HELL is keeping her?" Kevin groaned.

"Who?" asked Jessica.

"Monica. I want to go home."

"I'm here." Monica walked up to the pickup, struggling to hold the jerry can in her two hands.

Nate took the can and placed it in the bed. He then knelt before Monica and raised his right hand. "Good job."

Monica smiled and gave Nate a high five. "Thanks."

Nate stood. "We're done for the night. I'll drop you off—"

Fred's barking cut him off. The dog hung out of the passenger window, his tail curled under his body, focused on something behind them.

"What's wrong, buddy?"

Carissa pointed down the street, her hand shaking. "He's barking at them."

The group turned at the sound of squealing coming down

the street. A pack of zombie rats raced toward them, only two hundred feet away.

"Get in the back of the pickup. Now!"

The kids jumped in, Alanna and Myles assisting the smaller ones before climbing in themselves.

As they did, Nate reached into the back, unscrewed the lids on four of the jerry cans, and tossed them onto the street ten feet behind the vehicle. Gasoline poured from the open containers. The rats had closed to within fifty feet, their squealing growing more frantic as they neared their food.

Removing the lighter from his pocket, Nate flicked the flame on and held it near the gasoline. A wall of flame erupted between Nate and the rats, slowing them down. Nate climbed into the driver's seat, started the engine, and sped away. Glancing in his side mirror, he noticed the pack swarm around the flames and give chase. Fred jumped on Alanna's lap and stuck his head out the window again, defiantly barking at the rodents.

Jessica centered her face in the open window on the cab's rear. "What are we going to do?"

"Find a safe place."

"Where is that?"

Nate shrugged.

"The pier," said Alanna. "I have a boat ready so we can escape."

Nate looked over at her. "Are you serious?"

"I need to keep the kids alive."

He patted Alanna's shoulder. "Good girl."

Nate increased speed and headed for the pier.

BRAD AND SADIE lay in the bed, cuddling after being intimate. The bedroom window was open, letting the cool breeze in.

Sadie lay her head on Brad's chest and sighed contentedly.

"Are you tired?" he asked.

"Happy." She kissed his abs. "I finally feel like I'm alive again."

"Same."

They lay beside each other until a familiar sound shattered their happiness.

The distant squeal of zombie rats.

Sadie's eyes opened. Her body trembled. "No, no, no."

Brad jumped out of bed and ran over to the window. The squeals grew in volume, occasionally interrupted by the screams of a resident being eaten alive. Two blocks away, scores of rats emerged from the shadows and passed under a streetlamp, their decayed forms visible in the light.

Moving back to the bed, Brad slid on his underpants and trousers. "Hurry up and get dressed. We need to get out of here."

Sadie sat up on the mattress and held her knees against her chest. "No."

"What?"

"I'm not going anywhere."

Brad stared at her. "Are you serious?"

She nodded. "I suffered too much in those first years after the outbreak. I'm tired of running. It's over for me. I'm staying here."

Brad picked up his shirt. "But we can make it if we run now."

Sadie shook her head. "I'm done."

Brad paused. Part of him wanted to continue fighting to survive despite the past five years. The other part could not leave Sadie. He had lost too much during the original outbreak to lose everything that mattered to him again.

Throwing the shirt back onto the mattress, Brad crawled into bed. Wrapping his arms around Sadie's shivering body, he pulled her close.

"Whatever happens, I'm not leaving you."

"Are you sure?" Sadie's voice croaked as tears flowed down her face.

"I couldn't survive without you."

ETHAN STOOD ON the roof of City Hall, the collapse of Nahant taking place beneath him.

The pack moved through the neighborhood as it spread across the island. Three houses down on the right, a mother and her teenage daughter rushed out of the back door into their yard, hoping to escape. They did not stand a chance. The daughter stumbled, collapsing to the ground, crying out when she hit the grass. Spinning around, the mother ran back to help. As she lifted her daughter, rats swarmed over them, covering the mother and daughter. Their agonized death screams could barely be heard over the frenzied feedings of the rodents.

Between witnessing the community being ravaged and listening to the frantic communications from Roberta, the sheriff, and his deputies, Ethan realized the end was imminent. The rats had outsmarted him and figured a way around Nahant's defenses. This was the second time his world crashed around him, the second time he failed to protect the ones he cared for.

His will to continue the fight drained from him.

Ethan removed the two-way radio from his belt and tossed it over the side into the pack surrounding city hall. Heading down to his office, he closed the door and sat at his desk. Opening the lower drawer, he removed the bottle of Jack Daniel's, a glass tumbler, and one of the cigars Nate had gifted him. He peeled off the cigar's plastic wrapper, bit off the end, and placed it between his lips. Pulling a lighter from his pocket, he lit the tip until it glowed red, then inhaled, allowing the smoke to fill his mouth. Reaching over, he unscrewed the top of the whiskey bottle and filled the tumbler, gulping down three mouthfuls. The alcohol burned going down, but Ethan did not mind. He took another puff of the cigar.

If Ethan was going to die, at least he would die happy.

LIZ AND THE kids had been stuck in the fallout shelter for over fifteen minutes. Terror filled the kids' eyes as they listened to the rats frantically chewing and clawing at the steel door and concrete walls to get at the food inside, the constant noise reverberating within its confines. The four humans sat huddled in the far corner, Liz cuddling the kids who shook in terror.

"W-when will they break in?" stammered a terrified Debbie.

"They won't." Liz prayed she was not lying. "Rats can't eat through concrete and steel."

"But they're zombie rats," said Sean.

"It doesn't matter. Their teeth are not strong enough to chew their way into the shelter."

Though she refused to admit it, Liz worried that thousands of living dead rodents tearing at the concrete would eventually chew their way through. If they did, Liz had no way to rush the kids to another safe—

Myeong-hwa suddenly sat up straight. "Listen."

"I don't hear anything," Sean replied.

"That's what I mean. The rats have stopped trying to break in."

Liz's eyes widened. The noise had stopped. Hope surged through her. Did the rats finally give up and move on, or were they waiting outside for their food to come out? One thing Liz knew for certain, she would not risk testing the latter theory.

Myeong-hwa's eyes darted from the door to Liz. "We should get out of here while we have the chance."

"It's better that we wait," Liz answered calmly. "The rats

are nearby. If they see us, they'll try to get in again. Let's wait a bit before leaving."

"I'm bored," Sean whined.

Debbie sagged her shoulders. "Me, too."

"Miss Liz, read to us," suggested Myeong-hwa.

"I don't have any books with me." Liz clapped her hands together. "How about we sing?"

All three kids became excited at the idea. Liz began singing "Hakuna Matata" from *The Lion King.* The kids joined in, holding hands and swaying back and forth. The longer they sang, the more joyous they became. Liz smiled, glad that they were having a good time. They survived the second zombie outbreak.

Liz had no idea how wrong she was.

Fallout shelters built in the 1960s were equipped with manually operated, hand-cranked pumps to let in oxygen. When such shelters were no longer used for their intended purpose, the pumps were removed to create space. However, the air ducts used to transfer oxygen remained in the walls.

A lone rat wandered up to the second floor, running from classroom to classroom in search of prey. As it ran down the corridor, it passed the grate leading to the shelter and stopped, catching a familiar scent.

The smell of food.

Squealing at the top of its rotted lungs, the rat called out to the rest of the pack.

Ears perked up, homed in on the location, and swarmed upstairs, converging on the grate. One by one, the rodents climbed onto one another, creating a pile of moving, dead flesh. When the pile reached the grate, those on top chewed through the drywall surrounding the screws holding the grate in place. The screw on the right popped free first, causing that side of the grate to slide down, creating a path. With another loud squeal, one rat dived through the hole, sliding down the vent until it hit the grate to the shelter, hundreds of others following.

A LOUD CLANG interrupted the singing.

Debbie glanced up. "What was that?"

Sean narrowed his eyes. "What was what?"

"That noise."

"What noise?"

A second clang resounded from the grate, this time accompanied by a squeal.

"Shit!" Myeong-hwa jumped up. "They're coming down the air vent!"

"Get back against the wall."

Liz climbed to her feet, rushed over to the steel door, and spun the ship-style wheel. With luck, they could sneak out before the rats breached the air vent. Shoving the door open, she froze.

The rats had stopped attempting to break into the shelter but had not left the building. Several hundred of them still wandered the corridor. On hearing the creaky hinges of the steel door and detecting the smell of food, all of them rushed toward the shelter. She knew they could never make it out without getting eaten alive. She made a quick decision. Slamming the steel door shut and securing it, Liz prayed the grate would hold.

"Why did you close the door?" asked Debbie.

Sean pointed to the wall. "There are rats in the vent."

Liz forced a smile. "Don't worry. It'll hold. Now let's cuddle together and keep warm until they're gone."

The three kids joined Liz on the floor, knowing she had lied to them, but forgiving the adult because she had done it to protect them. Myeong-hwa sat on Liz's left, Debbie and Sean on the right. The kids closed their eyes, fighting back tears.

Liz focused her gaze on the wall. The frenzied squeal of the pack became overbearing, blocking out the sobs and heavy breathing of Liz and the kids. As more and more rats filled the vent, the weight increased, pushing against the grate. The metal bent outward about an inch, and the screws strained against the holes in the wall. They only had sec—

The grate ripped off the wall and clattered to the floor, followed a moment later by the thumping of zombie rats falling onto the concrete. The kids winced and hugged each other tight, waiting for the inevitable. Without hesitation, the rats swarmed toward their prey.

Liz closed her eyes tight and prayed the end would be quick.

GINA STOOD ON the top of the hill in front of Fort Ruckman's fire control tower, frozen in place from shock and fear.

She had experienced unimaginable horrors during the outbreak, events that she miraculously survived that would haunt her memories forever. Yet witnessing the nightmare play out from a distance was terrifying on a different level.

Rats flooded across Nahant like a tidal wave, their squeals audible even at this distance, mixing with the death knells of the locals. Of the people she knew. People she formed bonds with over the last few months. Men, women, and children whose efforts to start a new life after the apocalypse would soon end in agonizing deaths.

Gina watched Sheriff O'Brien and Donnelly racing through the streets, warning the locals to escape. Nate's pickup truck heading toward their pier. Panic-stricken people running through the streets in a vain attempt to escape, being overrun and outflanked by the living dead. Only a handful escaped the flood of decayed vermin, merely delaying the inevitable.

Glancing over her shoulder, Gina noticed the ocean was only a few hundred feet away at the bottom of the hill. The rats had not reached this part of Nahant yet. She contemplated trying to escape. If she moved now, she would have a good chance of making it. However, not being a good swimmer, Gina doubted she would make it to Swampscott. She opted to stay put, praying the rats would not notice her.

NATE SPED DOWN Willow Road and swerved into the pier's parking lot. From the back came the rattling of jerry cans sliding across the bed and slamming against the sides, accompanied by the kids' yells as they were tossed about. Even Fred barked at the sudden turn.

"Slow down," warned Alanna. "We're fucked if we crash."

"We're fucked if we don't get to the pier before the rats do."

Nate drove up to the shoreline, slowing down so he could park the pickup with the rear perpendicular to the pier. Without shutting off the engine, he jumped out and helped the kids onto the ground. As he helped the last one down, Fred moved alongside Nate and growled. Nate spun around.

The rats ran down Willow Road and swarmed into the parking lot.

"We're dead," said Heather, clutching the teddy bear against her.

"We're not." Nate removed two jerry cans from the pickup's bed. "Get to the boat. I'll slow them down."

Alanna ushered the kids down the pier, stopping Kevin and Jessica as they passed. "The key to the ignition is under the driver's seat. Start the boat and be ready to leave. If something happens to Nate and me, don't hesitate to go."

"But what—" began Jessica.

"No buts." Alanna leaned forward and hugged the siblings. "Take care of them."

Nate opened the two jerry cans and spread the gasoline in a

line surrounding the entrance to the pier. Fred moved forward a few feet and barked as the pack drew closer.

"Someone get Fred to the boat," Nate yelled.

Myles rushed forward and picked up the dog, grunting at his weight. Fred struggled to break free but gave in, then began whining for his master.

Once the kids were out of the parking lot, Alanna removed a jerry can from the truck and emptied its contents across the end of the pier, soaking the wood.

Nate finished pouring the gasoline as the pack drew near. Removing his lighter from his pants pocket, he flicked it on and tossed it on the gasoline, instantly creating a flaming barrier.

Frantic for food, the pack ran through the flames. Several caught fire. Most did not.

Several hundred swarmed over Nate, knocking him over. He fell against the rear wheel of the pickup, screaming in agony as the rodents began ripping into his body. He frantically brushed them off. For everyone tossed aside, another took its place. Forcing himself to stand, Nate lunged forward, tossing himself onto the flames, killing several hundred rats in the process.

The rest of the pack headed for the pier.

Alanna searched her pockets but had nothing to light the gasoline she had poured. Some of the rats bypassed Alanna and raced for the boat. Most attacked Alanna, including a dozen rats on fire. Alanna knew she would soon be dead. To save her kids, she tossed herself on the gasoline-soaked pier.

The wood ignited, creating a three-foot-long barricade. Those rats who attempted to cross burst into flames. Only a dozen made it past the flames and continued down the pier. As the fire consumed Alanna, her final thought was a prayer that the kids would survive.

HEATHER, CARISSA, AND Monica reached the pontoon boat

first, climbing on board and waiting for the others. Myles followed a second later, taking a seat near the front. He placed Fred on the deck but held the dog's collar so it didn't run off to be with Nate. They heard Kevin and Jessica approaching.

"Alanna!" Monica screamed as she watched the rats cover her. She jumped off the boat and started to run back.

Kevin ran past her. Jessica stopped Monica, turned her around, and pushed her back to the boat.

"We have to save Alanna," Monica cried.

"She's gone." Once on deck, Jessica dropped to her knees and hugged the girl, both of them crying over their loss.

Kevin sat in the driver's seat and rummaged around beneath the cushion until he found the key. He slid it into the ignition, turned it to the right, and pressed the START button. The engine roared to life. He glanced over his shoulder.

"Someone detach the dock lines."

Jessica and Monica jumped up, detached the two dock lines, and threw them onto the pier.

"Clear," Jessica called out.

"Hurry up." Carissa pointed at the rats rushing down the pier. The closest was fifty feet away.

Kevin shoved the throttles to full and spun the wheel to the right, rapidly pulling away from the pier. When twenty feet away, he turned in his seat. The rats reached the end of the pier. Most dove into the water to catch up with the boat, but they fell far behind.

Jessica stepped up to Kevin and spoke softly. "What now?"

"We'll circle around Nahant and head north. There's a military base in Salem."

As the boat pulled away, Myles released Fred. The dog rushed over to the end of the boat, looked at Nahant, and whimpered. Myles joined Fred, sitting beside the dog and trying to comfort him.

O'BRIEN STOPPED THE Land Rover when Kathy and her son Conner, the rat expert, ran in front of the vehicle, waving down the sheriff. He and Donnelly stepped out.

Kathy raced around to the driver's seat. "Help me."

"There's nothing we can do to stop the rats."

Her eyes were glazed with fear. "What can I do?"

"Head to the beach," suggested Donnelly. "From there you can swim to safety."

"Thank you." Kathy grabbed Connor's hand, and the two ran off, heading into Nahant rather than the beach.

A second later, she screamed as a pack of rats swarmed over them.

"It's over," sighed O'Brien.

"What do we do now?"

O'Brien removed his revolver. "I'm not going down without a fight."

Donnelly slid his revolver from his holster and joined the sheriff. As the pack approached, they killed as many rats as possible before being overwhelmed.

ETHAN WAS HALFWAY through his cigar and two-thirds of the way through his whiskey when he heard the glass doors to city hall shatter, followed by the sound of stampeding rodents heading down the corridor. A minute later, they began chewing their way through the wooden door of his office.

Picking up the bottle of Jack Daniel's, Ethan swigged down the rest of the bottle. With luck, he would be drunk enough that he wouldn't feel his skin and organs being stripped from his body.

Thanks to the alcohol, Ethan was able to push all the negative thoughts from his mind, focusing on his family and all the good times they had together. He could almost feel his wife's arms hugging him and his kids' laughter as they played together in the backyard. Despite his impending death, Ethan smiled.

The wooden door cracked open, accompanied by the hungry rats' intense squeals. Ethan took another long swig of whiskey and a final puff on his cigar as the pack swarmed into his office and across his desk. It would be over soon.

Ethan closed his eyes and thought one final time of his family.

"We'll be together soon."

BRAD HEARD THE intense squealing as living dead rats surrounded their house, followed a few minutes later by the shattering of glass as they broke through the patio doors. The noise of thousands of scampering feet came from the stairs.

Sadie sobbed loudly, holding Brad so tight he found it difficult to breathe.

The rats began chewing their way through the bedroom door.

Leaning over, Brad opened the drawer to his dresser and removed the 9mm Makarov semi-automatic pistol he kept for emergencies.

"I love you," he whispered to Sadie.

"I love you, too," she cried.

Brad placed the gun inches from her head and pulled the trigger. Sadie's blood and brains splattered over him, making him gag. At least he spared her from the upcoming misery.

The bottom of the door burst open, and rats swarmed in, most of them heading for the bed. A few jumped onto the bureau, shoving the mermaid statue onto the floor, where it shattered.

Brad placed the barrel of the Makarov under his chin and pulled the trigger.

VINNIE RAN AT full speed toward the shore, his attention focused ahead of him on the lookout for danger. Martha Lee stayed a few feet to the rear, clutching Little Vinnie against her chest. They paused when they reached Marginal Road. Stony Beach sat in front of them.

"We made it."

Martha Lee caught her breath. "Thank God."

A blood-curdling scream from behind caused them to turn around.

Three men and a woman followed a few hundred feet behind them. The pack gave chase. Two of the men and the woman ran between a pair of houses along the shore. The third man swerved to the right and made his way through the trees.

Suddenly, the woman tripped and crashed to the ground. Both men stopped, the taller of the two going back to help. The two were quickly overwhelmed. Turning around and running, the second man barely made it three feet before being taken down. By going on another route, the third man escaped death and rushed toward Marginal Road.

Vinnie put his hands on Martha Lee's shoulders and gently pushed. "Run!"

The two raced down to the beach, finding it difficult to run on sand. They each stumbled several times, thankfully righting themselves before falling. When twenty feet from the water, a voice called out.

"Wait for me."

The survivor crossed Marginal Road and jumped onto the beach. Rats breached the incline a second later. He barely made it five feet before a dozen rats jumped on his back, knocking him over. He screamed as the rodents chewed into his flesh, thrashing around in a futile attempt to throw off the vermin. His anguished cries were stifled when he was buried under hundreds of rats.

The rest of the pack swarmed around the feeding frenzy and rushed down the beach.

Vinnie headed for the shore. Martha Lee already stood in the ocean, the water up to her waist.

"Why are you waiting?"

Fear distorted Martha Lee's face. "I'm not a good swimmer. I'm afraid I'll drop Little Vinnie."

Stephen took the baby, held it tight in his left hand, and began swimming with his right, keeping the child above the surface. Little Vinnie wailed, exciting the rats whose squeals increased in intensity. Martha Lee joined him.

The couple had swum fifty feet when they heard splashing from the shore. Several of the pack had dived into the water and closed in on the couple.

THE PONTOON BOAT had circled around Nahant and moved along the east coast. Heather moved to the rail and pointed toward Stony Beach.

"There are people in the water being chased by rats."

Except for Kevin, who piloted the boat, the rest of the kids joined her.

Jessica looked at the others. "We need to help them."

Monica shook her head. "We'll never make it in time."

"We have to at least try," said Myles.

Everyone stared at him. It was the first time the teenager had spoken since he joined the group. His voice was low and firm, sounding more like an adult than a teenager. Myles continued.

"None of us would be alive today if Alanna had not taken risks to save us. We'd be dishonoring her memory if we allow them to die without at least trying to save them." When no one argued, Myles turned to Kevin. "Let's get them."

Kevin spun the pilot wheel and turned the boat toward shore, rapidly closing the distance. Myles and Carissa stepped over to the opening in the guardrail. The rest of the kids kept watching the rats close in on the couple.

As the boat drew within twenty feet of the couple, Monica called out. "The rats are only a few feet away. We're not going to make it."

"Yes, we will." Kevin turned the pilot wheel to the left, moving away from the couple.

"THERE'S A BOAT coming to save us." A tone of hope edged Martha Lee's voice.

Vinnie knew otherwise. The rats were too close. When the boat swerved away, he made the decision to pass the baby back to his wife and swim into the pack, sacrificing himself—

The boat suddenly veered right. For a moment, Vinnie thought the driver was heading toward him and Martha Lee. He then realized it targeted the rats.

Rushing past the couple, the boat ran over the rats, crushing several beneath the pontoons. The propeller chewed up the rest, leaving a pool of congealed blood and decayed flesh floating on the surface.

Making a U-turn, the boat slid up beside the couple and stopped. Two teenagers reached over the side, the girl taking Little Vinnie and the boy helping Martha Lee aboard. He then knelt down and extended his hand to Vinnie. The moment Vinnie was aboard, the driver, another teenager, throttled the engines and raced away from Nahant.

Martha Lee took Little Vinnie and hugged him, her gaze focusing on the two who had helped them aboard. Tears flowed down her cheeks.

"Thank you for saving us."

"Don't mention it. We couldn't let you die." The boy

paused. "Were any of you bitten?"

They shook their heads. Martha Lee sat down on one of the benches, cradling Little Vinnie, who cried at the top of his lungs.

"Shh, honey. It's okay. You can stop crying. We're safe."

The baby continued to wail.

A girl around seven years old stepped up. She held a dirty, dried blood-covered teddy bear. To Martha Lee's surprise, the girl held out the teddy bear.

"Maybe this will comfort him."

On seeing the teddy bear, Little Vinnie stopped crying and reached out. The girl gave it to him. Little Vinnie squealed with delight and hugged it.

"Thank you," said Martha Lee.

The girl smiled. "You're welcome."

Vinnie stepped to the boat's stern and stared at Nahant, which quickly receded in the distance. He closed his eyes and thanked God that they had survived.

ROBERTA AND USMAN stood atop the lift, staring out over Nahant, their despair deepening.

The only noise emanating from the island was the intense squealing of the living dead rats as they devastated the once-thriving community. No more relays coming from the two-way radio. No more gunshots. No more screams as residents died. The community of Nahant no longer existed; it had joined Revere as a victim of the second zombie outbreak.

"What now?" asked Melissa.

Usman looked over the railing. A bunch of zombie rats milled about, stripping the carcasses of Roger and Dylan of what little tissue remained. "We have to stay here until someone rescues us."

"I meant, where will they go next?"

"There's a community a few miles north in Swampscott, and you have the military installations in Salem."

"Then this is not over."

Usman shrugged. "That depends on how the military responds."

CHAPTER FIFTEEN

DENNING AND HER crew departed Salem shortly before dawn so she could fly over Boston to ensure the ZED outbreak had not spread any further. They arrived as the sun crested the horizon.

"Do you see anything?" she asked.

"Nothing out of the ordinary." Libby lowered his binoculars. "Typical wasteland, but no rats."

"Same here," replied Plati.

Denning flew toward the Logan Airport post of the Boston ZCZ, then continued on to Winthrop. Nothing had changed since their last sortie. Both areas remained a wasteland with scores of ZED rats still milling aimlessly around both locations.

Continuing on to Revere, the crew was shocked by the devastation that the community had suffered. The nursing home and condo had been ravaged, with most of the windows shattered. A few bodies lay strewn around the buildings and streets, the skeletons stripped clean of every living tissue. Nothing living could be seen, just scores of ZED rats rummaging through the carnage.

"Jesus," Libby muttered through the intercom. "They're wiping out everything in their path."

Denning said nothing. She continued flying along the coast road, crossing over into Lynn. The scattered rats roaming the area confirmed they were tracking their path.

"Have any moved inland?" asked Denning.

Libby shook his head. "Not that I can see."

"Good. That'll make it easier to take them out."

Plati tapped Denning on the shoulder and pointed straight ahead. "There's a bunch of ZEDs on that outcrop of land."

Denning veered right, hovering over the outcrop. Approximately a hundred ZED rats milled around. "What's this place called?"

Plati checked the map. "Lynn Heritage State Park."

"Radio headquarters what we've seen so far. Tell them we're still searching for—"

Libby interrupted the pilot with a single word across the intercom. "Fuck."

"What's wrong?"

"I found the pack. They're on Nahant."

Turning the Huey right, Denning flew over the bay. As the helicopter approached the island, a stunned silence filled the cabin.

Tens of thousands of rats covered Nahant from the causeway to the southern tip. The island appeared as if a charnel house had exploded, with dozens of bodies stripped of all their flesh and organs scattered around. ZEDs ran in and out of residences and local structures. A fire burned along the pier on the island's southern tip. The only thing none of them spotted was humans. Denning assumed no one made it out alive.

"Do you want me to call it in, sir?" asked Plati.

Denning nodded reluctantly.

As the lieutenant radioed in the coordinates, Denning watched the rats worm their way across Nahant. Two communities and a military installation wiped out in less than twenty-four hours. She could not imagine how many people were lost in this second outbreak.

COLONEL ANDREWS STRAPPED himself into the ejection seat of his FA-18 Hornet, pulling the integrated torso harness tight around his chest and the restraints around his legs to secure him in place. After connecting his oxygen and G-suit, the colonel adjusted the avionics, checked the flight controls, and verified the weapon systems.

He thought this pre-flight check was a bit of an overkill. They were flying to a target only sixty miles away at an altitude no higher than ten thousand feet and attacking an enemy that had no means of fighting back. However, protocol took precedence over everything else.

The morning mission briefing verified that the main pack of ZED rats had congregated on Nahant, where a community had been established nearly a year ago. Based on the devastation the rats inflicted on Winthrop and Revere, command assumed no one survived on Nahant. Even if some of the residents miraculously made it through the night, too many lives would be lost in a rescue attempt. The President had decided to eradicate the threat before the infection spread any further.

The colonel glanced up as he heard the roar of the C-130's four turboprop engines. The aircraft barreled down the runway before going airborne. The second of the ten transports pulled off the tarmac onto the runway, prepping to take off. The Hercules were responsible for eliminating the source of the threat. Once they had completed their mission, the Warthogs and Hornets would eradicate the ZEDs.

Andrews checked his watch. This should all be over in two hours.

"SIR, I FOUND two survivors." Libby lowered his binoculars, leaned forward, and pointed to the far end of the causeway. "Down there, on top of the elevated lift."

Denning looked in that direction, spotting a man and a woman atop the lift, waving frantically. "Let's rescue them."

She turned the Huey to the right and flew along the causeway.

As they approached, Plati warned, "Be careful. There's a bunch of ZEDs on the ground."

"I don't plan on landing." Denning turned to Libby. "I'm going to hover over the lift. Help the survivors on board."

"Yes, ma'am."

Libby moved to the left door, attaching his gunner harness to the safety tether. Denning slowly maneuvered the helicopter until the landing skids hovered inches above the lift's guardrail. Libby climbed out, balancing himself on the skid.

"Your Uber is here," Libby joked as he extended his hand.

The woman reached out and clasped it. Libby could see her shaking from fear. He helped her aboard.

"Thank you." She hugged Libby.

"You're welcome." Libby pointed to the rear of the helicopter. "Take a seat in the back and strap yourself in."

As she did, Libby helped the man climb in. After offering his thanks, he immediately moved to the back and strapped himself in by the woman.

"We're all set," Libby told Denning. As the helicopter lifted off and headed out to sea, the sergeant focused on the couple. "Are you okay?"

"Yes," replied the man, who then offered his hand. "I'm Usman. This is Roberta. We've been trapped up there since the rats invaded. Thank God you showed up."

"You're lucky we showed up when we did."

Roberta scrunched her eyes. "Why?"

"The Air Force will be here soon to kill off the ZEDs."

GINA WATCHED AS the helicopter rescued Usman and Roberta. She jumped up and down, waving frantically to catch their attention, quickly realizing the crew would never spot her amongst the trees. When the helicopter headed out to sea, Gina raced down the hill toward the shore, hoping she could get there in time to be rescued.

THE HORNETS CIRCLED above Hull at nine thousand feet, the Warthogs doing the same at six thousand feet, waiting for the C-130s to launch their strike.

The voice of the C-130 squadron commander came over the radio. "Big Daddy to all units, we are ready to make our bombing run."

"ZED Killer to Big Daddy, roger that," responded Andrews. "Good luck."

"Alpha One's in hot."

The colonel watched as the first Hercules flew over Boston at an altitude of six thousand feet. Its rear ramp lowered. As it passed over East Boston, ZED Killer announced, "Three. Two. One. Kicking it out the back door."

The drogue parachute opened, pulling the MOAB and its platform off the transport. The platform separated and plummeted through the air. The parachute slowed the bomb's descent, giving the C-130 time to escape the blast zone. When the MOAB reached an altitude of ten feet, the eighteen-thousand-pound warhead containing the H6 explosive composed of cyclotrimehylene, aluminum, and TNT detonated. The yield was equivalent to eleven tons of TNT.

A fireball expanded through the blast zone, billowing through the terminal and surrounding buildings and flowing through the sewers, setting fire to everything within range. Those ZEDs not incinerated were exterminated when the accompanying high-pressure shock wave slammed into them, crushing the rats. A large cloud of billowing white smoke mushroomed over East Boston, marking the end of any ZEDs in the area.

Three minutes later, the second C-130 moved in, repeating the same procedure against South Boston, with the same devastating results. The entire operation took slightly more than half an hour. When the last C-130 departed the area, devastation had been wreaked against downtown Boston, the South End, the West End, the North End, Back Bay, Fenway/Kenmore, Beacon Hill, and Charlestown. Nothing within the city, living or living dead, survived the bombing campaign.

"Big Daddy to ZED Killer, our part of the operation is complete. The show is now yours."

"ZED Killer to Big Daddy, roger that," replied Andrews. "ZED Killer to Black Widow, you may proceed."

"Black Widow to ZED Killer, roger that," replied Major Vassallo, the female commander of the Warthog squadron. "You heard the CO. It's time to fry some ZED ass."

The Warthogs broke away one at a time and headed toward Boston, with Vassallo taking the lead.

"Bravo One's in hot."

The aircraft flew over Winthrop, where the Logan Airport ZCZ housing once stood. The aircraft descended to an altitude of one thousand feet.

"Fox One and Fox Two away."

The pilot released the Warthog's two BLU-96 fuel-air explosives (FAE) at five-second intervals over the west coast of the peninsula. Each BLU-96 contained two explosives. The first detonated, bursting open the fuel container. The fuel mixed with the atmospheric oxygen, spreading across the west coast, flowing along the streets, and seeping into buildings and sewers. Three seconds later, the second explosive detonated, igniting the fuel. A thermobaric flame wave erupted across Winthrop, incinerating everything within range. A moment after that, the second BLU-96 exploded. Between the expanding flame front and the pressure created by both FAEs, every ZED on the west side of Winthrop was eliminated.

Ten seconds later, another Warthog duplicated the attack

on the peninsula's east coast.

With their bombing runs completed, the two Warthogs circled back and flew over Winthrop again, wing to wing. As they passed over the peninsula, the pilots fired their GAU-8 Gatling-style guns containing high-explosive incendiary rounds, making two passes over the peninsula until their ammunition ran out, ensuring nothing survived.

"Bravo One and Two are off," announced Vassallo over the radio.

The next nine Warthogs performed identical cleansing operations along Revere Beach, the Lynnway, and Lynn Heritage State Park. When the last Warthog headed back to Pease, over ten miles of ZED-invested territory burned.

Vassallo's voice came across the radio. "Black Widow to ZED Killer, RTB."

"ZED Killer to Black Widow, roger that. Good job."

"Black Widow to ZED Killer, thanks. I doubt anything survived that."

With the Warthogs gone, the Hornets formed an attack line and headed toward Nahant.

GINA REACHED THE shore. By now, the helicopter had moved a few miles out to sea. She doubted they would be able to spot her from this distance, yet that did not prevent her from trying.

After several minutes of jumping and waving, an explosion erupted behind her. She spun around, stunned to see a large, white cloud billowing over Boston. A few minutes later, a second explosion detonated, sending another cloud skyward to mix with the dissipating remnants of the first. The rumblings coming from the south sounded like a war zone.

Gina climbed back up the hill to Fort Ruckman, growing concerned as more explosions rocked Boston. By the time she reached the top, military aircraft began dropping bombs on

Winthrop, generating massive fireballs that devastated the peninsula, then circling back and strafing anything that remained.

Panic set in when the operation began along Revere Beach and Lynn. The realization dawned on Gina that the military was taking out every location occupied by the zombie rats, which meant Nahant would be next.

And she was at Ground Zero of that attack.

With few options available, Gina raced to find safe refuge somewhere inside the fort.

"IT'S OUR TURN." Andrews paused. "We'll go in groups of two. Nahant is overrun with the ZEDs, and this is our only chance to stop the outbreak, so make sure every acre of the island is burned to the ground. Is that clear?"

The other eight pilots responded in the affirmative.

"Let's fry these ZEDs."

Andrews and his wingman made their bombing runs. As the two fighters approached the island, Andrews announced, "Charlie One and Two are in hot."

Both pilots began firing their nose-mounted M61A1/A2 Vulcan rotary cannons when they reached the southern shore, the six-barrel weapons peppering the island with over four thousand 20mm rounds per minute. With tens of thousands of rats racing through the streets, the island became a slaughterhouse. The rounds slashed through the pack, obliterating the rodents and tossing their shattered carcasses and gore into the air, the spinning sound of the rotary cannon being drowned out by the death knells of thousands of zombie rats meeting their demise. None of those caught in the barrage survived.

When the Hornets reached the coast, both planes dropped their BLU-98s at five-second intervals. Andrews' hornet shuddered as the FAEs exploded behind him. Fragmentation from the blast ripped into the pack up to four hundred yards away, adding to the carnage. The overpressure caused intense damage to those buildings within a half-mile radius, and the flames from the six weapons engulfed the southern portion of the island, incinerating those ZEDs not killed during the strafing run. What was not destroyed or killed by the original blast was devastated by the underpressure.

"Charlie One and Two are out hot."

As Andrews and his wingman veered right so the pilots could view the damage, the next two Hornets began their attack.

GINA CUDDLED IN the corner of the fire control tower's basement, her knees pulled against her chest, sobbing. Through the concrete walls, she heard explosions erupting along Revere Beach and Lynn and felt the concussions shaking the ground. She repeatedly mumbled the Lord's Prayer, praying to a God she had never believed in until now, asking to be spared from a fate that deep down she knew was inevitable.

Gina's spirits rose when the surrounding explosions ceased. She looked up at the ceiling and laughed. God did exist and listened to her prayers. Once she got off Nahant—

The roar of approaching jet engines shattered Gina's hopes. She screamed at the top of her lungs.

Explosions ignited outside. The overpressure wave reached the building, slamming against the exterior. Chunks of cement fell from the ceiling, none of them hitting Gina. Seconds later, the underpressure, or negative pressure, began, creating a vacuum and sucking the air back toward the blast. The falling cement shot across the basement and slammed into Gina, fracturing her skull and breaking her arm. Her eardrums shattered, a portion of her intestines ruptured, and her left lung suffered from pulmonary edema, causing blood to flow from the tissue and fill the sac. Unfortunately for Gina, the blast did not kill her. She screamed again, this time in pain, as the burning fuel flowed into the basement. Gina breathed deep, searing out her lungs, killing her instantly and sparing the young woman from the agony of burning alive.

THE ZOMBIE RAT king crouched on the roof of a pickup truck along the west shore of Nahant, watching its empire across the bay erupt into flames, all the territory the pack had conquered burning furiously.

The roar of approaching aircraft from the south attracted the rat's attention. It shifted to the left and watched as two fighters swept across the island, dropping six bombs that devastated the southern tip. It felt the searing heat from the flames, followed by the overpressure, and heard the tortured squeals of its pack being annihilated.

It sensed the end was inevitable.

Two more fighters swept over Nahant. The king rat stood on its rear legs and screamed in useless defiance as six bombs tumbled from beneath the aircraft, exploding around the large rodent.

It continued crying out as the flames incinerated its body.

THE PRESSURE WAVE from the first FAE blast on Nahant slammed into the pontoon boat, despite it being several miles offshore. The boat tilted ten degrees to port, knocking down several passengers and sending everyone sliding across the deck. Kevin had enough common sense to steer the boat to starboard so the stern pointed toward shore and pushed the throttle to full, increasing the distance from Nahant. The pressure from the next few blasts still reached the boat but posed no threat of capsizing the vessel.

"God damn," muttered Myles as he watched Nahant erupt in flames.

"Everything is gone," added Kevin.

"Not everything," said Carissa. "We're alive."

Myles nodded his consent. "Thank God."

Jessica pointed to their right. "Look."

A military helicopter approached from the north. When a few yards from the boat, the helicopter lowered its altitude. A man in a military uniform positioned himself in the opening, yelling to be heard over the rotors.

"How many survivors are on board?"

"Nine, including a baby," answered Myles.

"That's too many for us to carry. Sit tight. I'll call another chopper to rescue you. We'll wait nearby until it arrives."

Myles raised his arm and gave the soldier a thumbs-up.

Roberta moved into the opening and waved. "I'm glad to see you're all safe."

"It wasn't easy," yelled Myles.

"I don't see Alanna."

"She didn't make it."

Roberta's expression blanched. She sat back down.

The soldier leaned out again. "A chopper will be here within the hour."

Myles waved again. "Thanks."

As the helicopter moved a few hundred feet from the boat, Heather walked over to Vinnie and Martha Lee. She pointed to her teddy bear clutched in the baby's hands.

"He likes it."

Martha Lee smiled. "He does. Thank you again."

"You're welcome. Everything will be alright."

"I know."

Vinnie leaned over and hugged Martha Lee. "Thank God the military killed all the zombies."

EPILOGUE

Two Days Later

THE CHINOOK HELICOPTER circled around Boston as it approached Logan Airport. The crew had flown this route many times previously to provide supplies to the ZCZ guard posts. All of them were shocked at the effects of the bombing.

The already post-apocalypse atmosphere now included the effects of being firebombed into oblivion. Rusted vehicles were burnt out. The garbage and corpses littering the streets had been turned into ash. Abandoned buildings had become charred hulks. Even the iconic Prudential Tower and John Hancock Building were devastated. The Prudential Tower had collapsed from the fifth floor up. The few remaining windows in the John Hancock Building had been blown out, the shards mixed in with the ashes covering the street.

"Holy shit," said Corporal Thompson. "It looks like Tokyo after we firebombed it."

"Except in Tokyo, we used our weapons against people," replied Sergeant Devens. "This time all we did was fry some ZEDs."

"I hope we got them all."

The unit commander, Major Carlson, joined the conversation, speaking loud enough for the entire unit to hear him. "We did. Drones and choppers have been checking all the bombed-out areas for forty-eight hours and have spotted nothing moving. The outbreak has been contained. You ladies have nothing to worry about."

Carlson felt confident that they were safe. This was a milk run. The guard posts around the Boston ZCZ had been manned again twenty-four hours ago, except for the Logan site. Carlson's ten-man unit was assigned to check it out and determine what was required to get the location operational again. In, out, and done.

The pilot's voice came over the intercom. "We'll be landing in one minute."

Carlson stood. "Okay, ladies. Get ready to earn your pay."

The helicopter hovered over the runway, slowly descending until the wheels touched down on the tarmac. Carlson stepped over to the door and opened it, waiting several seconds to see if the noise attracted any ZED rats that might be hiding in the shadows. When nothing emerged, he spoke into the intercom.

"All clear."

The pilot shut down the engines. When the rotors stopped churning, Carlson stepped out, followed by his unit.

Charred skeletons were scattered across the airfield; the bones of the one closest to the container wall were shattered, indicating he must have fallen from the top. Nothing remained of the carcasses except tattered military uniforms and grizzle. Many of the bones had teeth marks chewed across them. Intermingled among the human remains were sores of shattered rat bodies. The flames generated by the MOABs had not reached the runways, having been absorbed by the terminal. However, the pressure wave had done its job.

The guard post seemed in good condition. Several of the cargo containers on the top layer of the inner wall had been pushed askew or knocked off onto the tarmac. At least from this side, the wall appeared intact and could easily be repaired if command wanted to. Though that possibility was fifty-fifty. The wall was built during the containment of Boston when zombies infested the city. Other than the recent rat ZEDs, no living dead had been spotted in months.

Still, better safe than sorry.

"Devens, Thompson, Higgins climb to the top of the wall and report back on any damage it took."

The three men saluted and headed for the ladder.

"Robson, Bellamah, you're with me. I want to check out that building." The major pointed to a metal shipping container with its door wide open.

A slight stench of decay came from inside the building. Robson and Bellamah unslung their AR-15s and held them in the high-ready position. Carlson withdrew his Glock from its holster, prepared to fire.

Stepping inside, they realized the stench came from a few ZED rats. The only other body belonged to the radioman, who lay in front of the console, stripped clean by the rodents. The microphone dangled near the floor.

Bellamah took the microphone and held it in his hand. "That explains why we never heard from them. The rats must have swarmed him before he could get out a message."

"Poor bastard." Carlson shook his head. "Check and see if the radio works. If it does, tell command things aren't that bad here, and we'll give them a full report once we return to base."

Carlson and Robson stepped outside and stood in front of the communication shack.

"It could have been a lot worse," said Robson.

"I thought it would be. We lucked out." The major nodded his head toward a lone cargo container near the wall. "Let's check that out."

The three soldiers assigned to check on the wall descended the ladder and approached Carlson and Robson as they reached the container. Robson began undoing the cam-action draw latch as the major greeted his men.

"How's it look?" asked Carlson.

"Not bad," replied Thompson. "Some are banged up a bit, but the wall should still hold."

"Good."

Clanging metal caught their attention as Robson finished

unlatching and swung the doors open.

No one expected three ZEDs in military uniforms to rush screaming from the container and tear apart the soldiers, beginning the third outbreak.

Thank you for reading *Ratpocalypse.* I hope you enjoyed reading this novel. If you like it, please use the QR code below to leave a review on Amazon. The more reviews a writer receives, the more exposure their book gets on Amazon, which means more readers can experience the adventure. It means a lot to us.

Acknowledgments

I've been working on *Ratpocalypse* for several months. It has been years since I've written about zombies, and I missed it.

A huge debt of gratitude goes to Dan Uebel and Doc Fried, my beta readers. They tore my manuscript to shreds, finding my inconsistencies and plot flaws. My books would not be as good as they are without them.

Special thanks to Connor, the son of my good friend Kathy. He has kept rats as pets for most of his life and has provided extensive first-person information about their behavior. I included him in this book as my way of saying thanks.

Unfortunately, I was unable to find veterans willing to discuss details on how to properly use C4 and on the destructive capabilities of MOABS and FAEs. I did a lot of research on these topics and am probably on the FBI's watchlist (if I'm not on it already). I apologize for any inaccuracies.

I want to give a nod of thanks to my pets who dominate my free time. Fred, AKA Turd Burglar, my stubborn Beagle-Bassett mix, is always with me when I write, and sometimes I spend more time keeping him out of trouble than I do at my computer. My cat Archer has discovered that my plugged-in laptop makes the perfect heating pad, so getting him to move is next to impossible. At night, while editing and managing social media, my other cat, Michonne, stands in front of my desktop computer, demanding attention. They make the writing process difficult, but it doesn't matter. When I'm done writing, they are there to provide unconditional love and relaxation.

The biggest thanks go to my readers, especially those who

have been with me from the beginning. Writing is the fun part of my job. I appreciate all of you who read my books and patiently wait for the next one. I have a lot of stories floating around inside my head, and am looking forward to sharing them with you.

About the Author

Scott M. Baker was born and raised in Everett, Massachusetts, and spent twenty-three years in northern Virginia working for the Central Intelligence Agency. He has traveled extensively through Europe, Asia, and the Middle East, incorporating many of the locations and cultures in his stories. Scott lives outside Salem, New Hampshire, with his dog Fred and two cats who treat him as their human servant.

In addition to *Ratpocalypse*, Scott is currently working on the third and final book in his *A World Gone Dark* trilogy, a post-apocalyptic series about a solar flare that wipes out all electronics worldwide, which is part of the multi-author Ravaged Skies series. He is also working to complete *The Chronicles of Paul* saga and is plotting out his next zombie apocalypse series. Previous works include the *Nurse Alissa vs. the Zombies* series, his most popular zombie saga; his Tatyana paranormal series, his second most popular saga; *OSS: Office of Supernatural Services*, about Allied intelligence officers versus Nazi occultism during World War II; *Operation Majestic*, his first science fiction novel described as *Raiders of the Lost Ark* meets *Back to the Future* – with aliens; *Frozen World*, his first non-zombie post-apocalypse novel; the *Shattered World* series, his five-book young adult post-apocalypse thriller; the *Rotter World* trilogy, his first zombie series; and *The Vampire Hunters* trilogy, about humans fighting the undead in Washington D.C.

Facebook:
facebook.com/groups/397749347486177

Amazon Author's Page:
amazon.com/stores/Scott-M.-Baker/author/B003N4U9BK

Twitter:
twitter.com/vampire_hunters

Instagram:
instagram.com/scottmbakerwriter

TikTok:
tiktok.com/@scottmbakerwriter

Blog:
scottmbakerauthor.blogspot.com

YouTube:
youtube.com/channel/UC5AyCVrEAncr2E0N5XoyUdg/featured

Wyrd Realities Homepage:
www.wyrdrealities.net

You can also sign up for Scott's newsletter, which will be released on the 1st and 15th of every month. He promises not to share your email with anyone or spam the recipients. The newsletter contains advance notices of upcoming releases and events, as well as short stories from the Alissa universe that will not be available to the public. You can sign up by going to the link below.

Newsletter:
mailchi.mp/0b1401f1ddb2/scott-m-baker-writer

www.ingramcontent.com/pod-product-compliance
Lightning Source LLC
LaVergne TN
LVHW010948110826
845149LV00015B/3255
9798988497394